THE POWER BILLIONAIRE

THE COMPLETE SERIES

Angelina Spears

ISBN-13: 978-1480211476

ISBN-10: 1480211478

Visit Web Site at http://www.angelinaspears.com/

CONTENTS

AUTHOR'S NOTE

The Power Billionaire: The Complete Series features all three stories of BBW erotic romance: CURVES, SUBMISSION AND PLEASURE, DOMINATED CURVES AND DESIRE, and SUBMISSION OF CURVES DESIRES.

If you enjoy plump women finally being able to explore their sexuality without any shame, you will lose yourself in the tale of Merrin Rexford and her extraordinary adventures. However, please note that this is a work of erotic fiction. It features consenting adults doing the sort of things consenting adults do behind closed doors.

Enjoy!

THE POWER BILLIONAIRE 1: CURVES, SUBMISSION AND PLEASURE

CHAPTER 1

The plane was crowded but not overly so. It was hard not to appear crowded in such a confined space. And then there's the fact that, well, I'm a little bigger than most women. That has a tendency to make the world seem smaller. I could hear people chatting animatedly about what they'd do once in Florida. Mostly they were eager to go on the beach and soak up the sun but a few children several rows back were talking about Mickey Mouse. They were in for a disappointment, I thought. We were heading to Fort Lauderdale, nowhere near the same vicinity as Orlando.

We hit some turbulence outside of New York but so far -- we were over Virginia now -- the ride was smooth. I was alone and more than happy for it. I had some reading to do, needed to catch up. Sure, I was only an administrative assistant at an engineering firm but the ability to do my job greatly improved when I was familiar with everything that was going on at the office.

"Excuse me, is this seat taken?"

The voice was deep and smooth and yet it had a melodious quality to it. I looked up to my left and found a tall man wearing an Oxford shirt and a dark sports jacket. He was looking at me with a faint, expectant smile.

"Uh, no."

My spirits literally fell. I'd been ecstatic at being seated alone in my row. I hated sitting by the window as looking out gave me nausea and the aisle seat was even worse since people kept bumping into me. Ever had a serving cart smash you behind the elbow? The middle seat was perfect, especially now with no one on either side. Being a plump woman, I loved having some breathing space. And yet, I couldn't hold my ground and turn the guy away. That was the story of my life, too nice for my own good. I had screwed myself into a long and uncomfortable flight.

"Thank you, so much."

His smile was broad, displaying perfect white teeth. I was instantly struck at how handsome he was. His wavy brown hair was just long enough to be fashionable while still being considered short. He was in his 30s, maybe a year or two older than I was, and I saw some thin lines framing his piercing eyes. It was as if he spent a lot of time outdoors and smiled often. I removed some documents from the aisle seat and he sat down.

"Did we pick you up on the way somewhere?" I asked. "Were you hitchhiking?"

He chuckled good-naturedly. "I was in first class. I was upgraded, I never travel first class. Now I know why. Got into a... well, let's just say it was a strongly worded argument. It was agreed by all parties involved that we'd all be better off if I made myself scarce. Thank you for rescuing me."

"Sure."

I went back to my engrossing literature -- a quarterly report on my company's operations in Singapore. I saw the words and numbers but they didn't register. I felt like the man was watching me.

"I'm sorry," he said. "I didn't introduce myself. I'm Grayson."

"Merrin Rexford."

He extended his hand and I shook it without thinking. Whereas my hand was cold and clammy, his was firm and

4

warm. He looked into my eyes and I had the impression he held my hand one or two seconds longer than customary.

"It's a pleasure to meet you, Merrin."

"You too."

"You're going to Florida on business?" He pointed at my documents to accentuate his point.

"No, I'm visiting my grandmother. She had a surgery last week, I'm going down there to help."

"That's nice of you. You must love her very much."

"She practically raised me, she used to live at home with me and my mom."

"That's really sweet."

Someone else saying that would have sounded insincere. But not him. I knew right away he really meant it. He was still staring at me and I became uncomfortable. I was always uncomfortable when I was the center of attention.

"Are you going down to Florida for business?"

"Yes, unfortunately. Have to meet some people, sign some papers. Not much time for the beach."

I nodded and looked back down at the document. It was important to minimize our conversation because it was only a matter of minutes until I said something stupid and made a world-class fool out of myself. I always did that, which probably explains why I was still single. He respected my choice and picked up a magazine from this seatback in front of him.

After several minutes, there was some sort of ruckus in the back. Determined footsteps from a flight attendant could be heard throughout the cabin.

"What are you doing? You can't be in there! That's designed for only one passenger at a time!"

A lot of people, those who were still awake even though it was barely noon, turned in their seats to see what was going on. It didn't take a genius to get the idea and I stayed put. Grayson turned to me with a slight grin.

"Sounds like some people found a way to make the time go faster."

"Yeah."

"Are you a member?"

"A member of what?"

"Of the Mile High Club."

"No," I quickly shot back.

"There's no shame in it, you know. I'm a member myself, got the paperwork and everything."

He stared at me again with that little smirk, like the world was just a big game and he knew how to play it. He was waiting for me to reply and so I purposely didn't.

"I could induct you, if you want. We members have this power."

"You mean me going with you in that tiny little bathroom?" I dropped my voice. "You mean me having sex with you?"

"You say that like I'm repulsive."

"No but..."

The truth was I was the one who was repulsive. With a body like mine, guys didn't usually line up to make my acquaintance.

"But what?"

Instead of admitting the truth, I decided on another angle. Perhaps my candor would shut him up.

"Airplane bathrooms were designed for supermodels and midgets. I have trouble fitting in there by myself so any acrobatics in there with someone else have to be ruled out."

Grayson's smile brightened up and he leaned toward me. He brought his mouth less than two inches from my ear. I could smell the pleasant aroma of his aftershave. It was intoxicating and I feared I had walked through a door I never should have opened.

"I like that the first thing that popped through your head was the logistics of the operation. I love that you actually haven't ruled out having sex with me."

"Well..."

"Would you like to, Merrin?"

"I thought we already established that it can't be done. Especially now that the stewardess has just put the bathroom on DEFCON 1."

Without warning, he placed his left hand on mine and stroked it gently. I looked into his eyes and he didn't flinch. What was happening?!

"There's more than one way to become a member of the Mile High Club. There are other things we can do."

He brought his face even closer to mine and I held my breath. His body heat made my heart lurch and then he pulled back. *Yeah, just like I thought.* It was all a big joke. He stood up and moved into the aisle. I was expecting him to walk back to wherever he had come from. He didn't. He reached up into the overhead luggage compartment and produced a blanket. He sat back down and spread the blanket over the both of us.

"You can't be serious," I whispered.

"I'm very serious."

He turned in his seat so he could face me. This at the same time served to block the view anyone could have of us. Then, holding on to the blanket, he put an arm behind my shoulders. It was very casual like we were on a couch but it was also extremely intimate.

"What's the craziest thing you've ever done, Merrin?"

Serving mashed potatoes with lobster was probably the height of my zaniness. He continued looking at me, waiting for an answer.

"I skinny-dipped in New Hampshire once."

While this was technically true, I failed to mention that the lake was deserted and it was in the middle of the night. There was nothing crazy about it.

"What do you say we up the stakes a little?"

CHAPTER 2

He leaned toward me like he had done before. This time he went all the way until his lips touched my cheek. He took his time giving me the softest kiss I'd ever had. To be frank, it was almost chaste but it was so drawn out that I felt a flash of heat traveling through my body. Then he went lower, giving me two more kisses on the neck.

"We can't do this," I said reluctantly.

"Of course we can. And we can do more too. Do you have any idea how excited you make me?"

Before I could answer, he took my hand and led it up his thigh. I should have resisted, I should've screamed with horror. I couldn't. I wouldn't! I let him bring me to his crotch and at once I felt a bulge.

"Can you understand what I'm talking about now?"

He moved my hand up and down and within moments I was flexing my fingers in concert, squeezing his hardness. This was definitely my new benchmark for zaniness.

"I want you to take it out, Merrin. I want you to play with it."

I was a strong woman. I'd never let a man tell me what to do before. I'd never been a pushover. But there was something about Grayson's voice, his commanding tone. He was giving me an order but I could sense he was still giving me a choice. No, it was more like a challenge. It was like I would be disappointed in myself if I didn't comply.

"What if we get caught?" I asked in a last ditch effort to keep my dignity.

"What are they gonna do, pull over and throw us out? Stop making excuses, Merrin. Don't act like you don't want to see what it's like."

He took his hand off mine and strangely I didn't pull back. I remained in place and after several seconds I resumed exploring his groin.

"Take it out. See how big you make me."

His eyes bored into mine and I was hypnotized. I found myself wanting to push the envelope, to overstep my personal boundaries. I was a staunch feminist and yet I couldn't deny that there was something electrifying about being giving orders. Perhaps, I thought again, it was the way his honeyed voice sounded. He was commanding me and at the same time I knew he wouldn't get mad if I didn't follow through.

That only made me want to do it more!

With my heart beating a mile a minute, I undid his pants and lowered his zipper. His member readily sprung up and I toyed with it while it was still encased in the silky boxers. I ran a digit up and down, letting my fingernail trace his length. He had to suppress a gasp.

"Touch it," he said. "Touch the flesh."

Thinking I was actually on the brink of insanity, I felt around his underwear until I found the fly. I twisted the fabric and made him poke through the hole. He abruptly felt longer, bigger. I felt his heat all over my hand.

As a teenager, a boy had wanted me to do this to him at the movies and I had walked out on him. When I had relations with a man, it was always pitch dark in the bedroom. I was such a prude. So why was I even doing this? Why was I breathing faster?

Why was I enjoying this so much?

I grasped his hardness and it filled my hand flawlessly. It was like picking up a tool you'd left out in the sun for too long. It was a wonder I didn't burn my hand. I stroked him languorously, holding his gaze to show him I wasn't some Goody Two Shoes afraid to explore her wilder side.

"Do you like that, Merrin? Tell me how it feels to touch a stranger in the middle of a crowded plane."

"You're evil," I replied with the hint of a smile.

"No, evil is what I'm about to do."

With that, he put a hand on my left leg. He went down my knee until he encountered the hem of my skirt and then he pulled it back up. His broad hand was surprisingly delicate against my smooth skin. His touch was light but agile enough as to not tickle me. He crept up my thigh and rubbed circles on the flesh.

"Oh..." I groaned, my eyes flickering.

The angle made it difficult for him to go any higher and I caught myself being disappointed. *Oh my God, I'm so bad!* A minute ago, I was thinking the whole situation was madness and now I was upset he couldn't reciprocate? Still, what he was doing to me was a hundred times better than what I would've expected. I stroked him faster, letting my fingers mold themselves to his girth.

"Merrin," he said, craning his neck so he could nuzzle my ear, making his warm breath give me goose bumps. "I want you to pleasure yourself."

"What?"

"I know how much what you're doing to me is turning you on. I want you to benefit as well."

"I... I can't. Not here."

"Hike up your skirt and pull your panties to the side. No, I have a better idea. Take off your panties completely."

"This is insane, Grayson."

"What's insane is how much you actually want to do this. Just give in to your desire. Are your panties moist yet? I bet they are. Wouldn't it feel better if you removed them? Wouldn't it feel great to pleasure yourself as you're pleasuring me? Do it, Merrin."

Why was he making so much sense? I did feel incredibly aroused. And who would know? Everyone was oblivious to us and we were covered with a blanket. It would be our secret. Truth be told, I needed this more than ever.

I let go of him and both my hands shot under my skirt. I found the waistband of my panties and tugged down as I rose off the seat a couple of inches. The fabric was warm as I pushed them down along my legs. I settled back into the seat with my balled up panties in my hand.

"Good girl. Doesn't that feel better?"

The fresh air hit me between the legs and sent shivers up my spine. Or maybe it was him? He took the underwear from me and I was frightened he would discover how moist they were. He smiled knowingly.

"You like this much more than you let on, don't you? Take me again."

As if in a trance, I did as I was told. I curled my fingers around him and resumed my stroking. He was throbbing in my hand and I couldn't help feeling pride that it was me who was causing this.

"Now it's your turn, Merrin. Spread your legs and touch yourself."

I found that I was in a hurry to comply. It had been a while since I'd had any real desire and even longer since I'd done anything about it. While I continued to rub his engorged manhood, I lowered my right hand to my apex. I was taken aback by the heat already emanating. I made abstraction of the fact I was essentially doing this in public and at last I made contact with my lips.

"Aagghhh..."

"I know the feeling," he whispered in my ear. "Do it, let your fingers run free."

Barely able to breathe, I cupped my mound before exploring the folds. Oh why had I waited for so long to do this? It was nuts to be doing this in an airplane! Yet was that why it felt so good? I toyed with myself faster, wanting more, and I simultaneously accelerated my movements on Grayson. He was leaking and I spread it around for lubrication.

"That's it, don't stop now. You're so close to becoming a junior member of the Mile High Club."

I didn't reply, I couldn't. I was mesmerized by my own brashness, my own pleasure. I was his plaything and I didn't care. It made the heat flare up my belly and I stroked faster, the both of us.

I felt him move but I was too scared to say anything. I was afraid he would put a stop to this for some reason. This was the kind of luck I was afflicted with. But no, what he did was wrap my panties around his shaft before putting my hand back on him.

"Go faster, Merrin. I'm close."

Indeed, I could feel him quiver under my fingers. He was swelling, his tumescence on the verge of eruption. I accelerated, put more pressure. This went for me as well. My hand was frantic between my legs as I craved relief.

"Oooohh..."

That's all he had time to say. He became taught, his whole body seemingly digging into his seat as he exploded. I kept on stroking him as he filled my panties with his jetting seed. At this point, neither of us cared if we were caught. He was lost in the moment and I was beaming at being responsible for it.

"Thank you," he said.

He put his hand on mine to slow me down. Good, now I could focus on myself. My fire was properly stoked and I was practically gushing. I closed my eyes as I made contact with my delicate button. Yes... so close... so close...

"Ladies and gentlemen," the captain began. "We will begin our descent into Fort Lauderdale-Hollywood International in just a moment. You'll be happy to know that we are on schedule and the weather is beautiful. Please prepare for landing."

I stopped cold. Everywhere around us people were moving, sorting themselves out, buckling up. A flight attendant began tramping down the aisle toward us, making sure everyone was following instructions.

"That's unfortunate," Grayson said.

"That's unfair."

He straightened up and I knew from his demeanor he was zipping up his pants. I saw him pocket my underwear which was just as well, I couldn't put them on again. How could life be so cruel? I'd taken so many risks, I'd been so close. Why was I being denied my much-needed release?

"We'd better remove the blanket before she takes it from us." He pressed his lips against my ear. "Before she smells the inebriating scent of your sex."

He kissed my cheek tenderly and sat up straight again. Not having a choice, I lowered my skirt and buckled up before allowing the blanket fall down.

"Once you reach your destination, when you finish what you started, I know what you'll be fantasizing about."

"What?" I asked.

"This."

He took my right hand, the hand I'd been masturbating with, and brought it to his face. He inhaled my shiny fingers before taking them into his mouth. He sucked them gently, making his tongue swirl around them, and then released me. The whole thing lasted no more than five seconds but it seemed like an eternity.

I wanted it to be an eternity.

* * *

I was on pins and needles until the plane came to a stop and we barely said two words to each other. He returned to first class before we deplaned and we made our way down the escalator into the baggage carousel. I had the misfortune of having a popular Samsonite suitcase so I had to keep my eye on the luggage as to not miss it. Grayson was on the other side.

"Huumm, so gorgeous..."

I looked up at the voice. It came from the middle-aged woman next to me. I followed her gaze and sure enough she was watching the man to whom I'd basically given myself.

"Oh what I wouldn't give to be the next Mrs. Holmes."

The woman was basically thinking out loud but I couldn't help joining the conversation.

"Excuse me, you know him?"

"Well, not personally. But everybody knows who he is."

"They do?" I asked incredulously.

"Why, that's Grayson Holmes! You know, the billionaire."

That's when it registered. Of course I'd heard of him, I might even have seen his picture before once or twice. My brain never made the association because on the one hand billionaires didn't fly coach and on the other I wasn't the sort of woman they usually talked to.

My suitcase swung by me and I hurriedly grabbed it before it was too late. When I looked up, Grayson was surrounded by people. There was a silver-haired man in a pinstripe suit, a bulky linebacker type in a charcoal suit, and a tall woman with auburn, chin-length hair. She was standing with her back to me and had her hand on Grayson's upper arm.

CHAPTER 3

That simple gesture made me positively angry. It wasn't jealousy but rather the fact that he already had a girlfriend and had deceived me for a quick sexual thrill. What a bastard! *Maybe I should confront him*, I mused. I could make a scene and truly embarrass him. These rich, famous people thrived on good publicity. I could wreck his reputation in less than a minute.

I was still making up my mind about it when he headed out of the terminal with his entourage. Against all odds, I was disappointed. He may have lied to me, may have cheated on his girlfriend, but it couldn't erase the fact that the flight had been one of the highlights of my life. *I should've known*, I thought. My life was destined to suck.

I snatched my suitcase and walked to the exit. There was a curtain of ice cold air between the two sliding doors and then heat and humidity assaulted my senses. I actually liked it. It was such a welcome change after the dreary New York winter. I looked left and right for a cab; most of them around here were white or turquoise which made it harder to spot, as opposed to the customary yellow.

"I beg your pardon, are you Ms. Rexford?"

I whipped around and faced a short Hispanic man in a dark suit.

"Yes, I'm Merrin Rexford."

"Your car is right this way."

"My car? What are you talking about? I'm just looking for a taxi."

"Well, I've been hired to take you anywhere you wanna go. My car is right here."

He pointed to a black stretch limo parked on the curb a few yards away. How...

"Let me help you with this," he continued as he took the suitcase from me.

I was about to resist and instinctively looked around to see if Grayson was in the area. No one else could have known my name and hired a driver. He was nowhere in sight. The thought of declining the offer on principle occurred to me. *That would show him*, I thought spitefully. But I was a practical girl. When you grow up in Brooklyn you learn never to refuse a free ride.

The driver put my luggage in the trunk and then opened the door for me.

"I'm going to Boca Raton," I said as I got in.

For the first time in several hours I thought of my grandmother, the reason I was here. She would certainly lift my spirits.

*　*　*

"Can I get you more cannolis? How 'bout some latkes, would you like some latkes?"

"I'm fine, Grandma. Thanks."

My grandmother, all 4'10" of her, was nothing if not cuddling. She made sure you ate until you burst and then got you an extra helping for good measure. It had gotten out of hand ever since she had discovered a place a couple of blocks away called World Deli. It had every ethnic dish on the planet and Grandma Edna was determined to sample them all.

"Eat, eat! You're so skinny, it's not healthy."

Did I mention how she was also losing her eyesight? To her, anyone who wasn't built like an opera singer was unhealthy. This was especially bewildering taking into consideration Grandma was rail thin. Fast metabolism, she called it.

"Dinner was delicious, thank you. But you shouldn't be running around like this. You're recovering from surgery, remember?"

"Surgery, schmurgey," she dismissed with a wave of the hand. "They removed my gallbladder, it's not like they gave me one of them sex change operations. Ever see one of those trans people? There was one on TV the other day, when I was playing bridge at Margaret Bielszowski's. Old Harry Meyerson kept commenting on how sexy she was. It took half an hour to explain to him he was looking at a man. What's a trans man, anyway? Is it a woman who's become a man or a man who went under the kitchen shears and became a woman?"

"I don't know, Grandma."

"Yeah, it's complicated."

I stood up and started clearing the dishes. She bounced up from her chair and planted herself next to me at the counter. She extended her neck like a prairie dog and I knew why too. She was adamant that whatever she didn't eat had to be boxed up for snacks the next day.

"You sure you don't wanna eat anything else, Merrin? I have some pickle soup I could reheat."

"We just had supper, Grandma. We just had dessert!"

"Oh? At my age you eat what you want when you want. Marvin Spoolstra's been eating cabbage rolls for breakfast ever since he found out he had gonorrhea."

I furrowed my brow and turned to her. "Isn't Mr. Spoolstra like 90 years old?"

"91," she corrected. "He's doing it like a rabbit now. He learned about sexting, they're all doing it now. Ever since old lady Claycomb started giving out them little blue pills, bingo night... well, it ain't just about bingo anymore. I think I might start some of that sexting. I gotta get me one of them little phones."

"Grandma, you know I'll be having nightmares from now on, do you?"

"Hey, a woman my age needs some good time. I'm very desirable, you know. I'm a few years shy of 80. They think I'm a babe."

"That you are, Grandma."

I kissed the top of her head and went to work on the

dishes. It felt weird to finish eating when it was barely five o'clock but after the midair ordeal I was hungry. My grandmother was a little eccentric but at least it kept my mind off the insanity from before. I finished cleaning up while she went to the living room to watch her shows. I was about to join her when there was a knock at the door.

"I'll get it."

"Let me know who it is and let them wait outside so I can freshen up."

I grinned at the shenanigans that had overtaken my grandmother's senior residential complex while I went to the door. I opened it and my smile vanished. Standing in front of me was Grayson Holmes.

"Good evening, Merrin."

"Who is it?" Grandma called from the living room. "Is it Bernie Renihan? Hold on, I'll get my good teeth."

I barely heard her scurry to her bedroom. My eyes were riveted to the billionaire before me. The cheating, lying, perverted billionaire.

"What do you want? And how did you even find me?"

"I got you a limo, didn't I? The driver was kind enough to tell me the address. This is where your grandmother lives?"

"What do you want?" I repeated.

"Are you still frustrated you didn't get to climax?"

Without a word, I slammed the door shut. I hated to admit it but the fact that I didn't get to cum like he did weighed on me. I had told myself I would find a private place to finish what I started but it was difficult with Grandma around. And when I thought of Grayson I couldn't keep his deception out of my mind. That just killed the mood.

I thought I was home free but the door wasn't actually slammed shut. His foot was in the way. He gently pushed the door open again.

"I'm sorry, Merrin. Can you give me a moment, please?"

"You lied to me."

"How did I do that? By not telling you my last name? That's not lying, that omission."

"You said you never travel first class."

"I don't, that's the truth."

"Bullshit. You're Grayson Holmes, you're a billionaire. You only travel first class."

"False. I never take commercial flights, I have a private jet. Therefore, I wasn't lying to you. I never fly first class."

"So you're gonna play with words now? Are you a lawyer?"

That made him smile. "They found a technical problem with my plane at the last minute so we had to go commercial."

"We, as in you and your girlfriend?"

"What are you talking about?"

"I saw her at the airport, that tall, beautiful skinny redhead with her hand on your arm. You weren't exactly pushing her way."

He was puzzled for an instant and then burst into laughter. "I'll have to tell my mom you called her tall, skinny, and beautiful, she'll fall in love with you for sure."

"Your mom?" I asked, the voice catching in my throat.

Was I making a fool out of myself? Again?

"Yes, Merrin. My mom. I flew down from New York with my parents. There's a political thing tonight at the family retreat. They said I had to be there so I came like a good son."

"Your mom? I... But... What... How come you were with me? You said you had an argument."

"Okay, so I lied a little." He leaned forward and got his head closer to mine. It wasn't too overt, just friendly. "I noticed you when we boarded. It took me an hour to find a way to talk to you. I had to pay the stewardess to allow me to sit next to you."

"Oh." It was all I could say.

"I'm sorry I gave you the wrong impression and I'm sorry I couldn't walk with you out of the airport. The truth is, I can't get you out of my head, Merrin. I want you to come to the party with me tonight. It'll be full of stuffy rich and boring people. I promise you'll have a lousy time but at least we'll be having a lousy time together."

For the first time I noticed he was wearing a finely cut

tuxedo. He didn't look like the bowtie type of person but it was uncanny how attractive he was dressed like this. *Batman, eat your heart out!*

"What do you say?" he whispered.

His explanation made me forget about my frustration. I had been a fool to peg him as a lying bastard. Why did I always react like my life was at the center of a bad sitcom? Then again, how couldn't I? It was impossible that a wealthy handsome man could ever be interested in me.

"I can't go to anything fancy, I have nothing to wear."

"That can be arranged. Just say yes."

He reached for my hand and I let him take it. He caressed my fingers slowly and gazed into my eyes. I had flashbacks of grasping his hardness, of feeling him pulsating in pleasure. Could that happen again? Could that happen inside of me?

"So," my grandmother said. "Is it for me?"

I turned and found her standing behind a corner, peeking at us. She had indeed put on her good teeth. They were overly straight and overly white.

"No, Grandma. This one's for me."

CHAPTER 4

We drove more than 20 miles north and it felt like nothing. Part of it was having him near me, his hulking presence a subtle reminder of what we had gone through on the plane. Another part of it was the vehicle. It was a dark Maybach, a car that made Rolls-Royce look like a run-of-the-mill junker. The passenger area was roomy and luxuriously appointed. I kept looking around like a teenage girl going to the prom.

We crossed the bridge and headed into Palm Beach which was built on a narrow barrier island. We zoomed through traffic and every car seemed to be a Ferrari or a Maserati. Anyone in a BMW or Lexus was slumming. We drove down to Worth Avenue.

"They call this the Rodeo Drive of Florida."

The street was lined with palm trees. Beyond them were elegant two-story buildings housing shops. I saw names like Ralph Lauren, Valentino, Lana Marks, Lacoste, Giorgio Armani, Louis Vuitton, Tiffany & Co., Brooks Brothers, and Salvatore Ferragamo. I could practically smell the money.

"Maybe we could stop by a mall somewhere," I said. "There's always something at Macy's that looks good and isn't liable to bankrupt a small country."

Grayson grinned. He didn't answer. The driver had his instructions and soon the car came to a halt in front of Gucci.

"You can't be serious."

"I'm very serious. I know you'll already be the most beautiful woman at the party. With the dress you pick out in there? You'll be the most beautiful woman in history."

He brought his head close to mine and our lips brushed. I was about to kiss him firmly when he moved aside and pecked my cheek tenderly. The chauffeur opened my door and I had no choice but to climb out.

"Good evening Mr. Holmes," a woman said opening the store door for us. She looked like a supermodel.

We went in and quickly two other salespersons came to us. Grayson mentioned we were going to a glamorous affair, as if his tuxedo didn't give it away, and the staff members went about showing me what they thought was suitable. They didn't even do a double take at my size. I was used to dismissing everything for fear it wouldn't fit me but they didn't bat an eye.

In the end, I chose a silk georgette halter dress. It was black with double velvet ribbon detail and a subtle ruffle neckline. I tried it on and it made the impossible of making me appear svelte.

"You look ravishing, Merrin."

After it was decided that we were settling on this one, a saleswoman cut off the price tag and I couldn't help myself from glancing at it. My heart nearly gave out.

"Grayson, it's $5,000."

"That's strange because it makes you look like $1,000,000. It must be you then."

He paid and we left the store. I was certain we were going to the party now but instead we went to Jimmy Choo so I could get some shoes even though mine were perfectly adequate. He made me choose black round-toe pumps that were actually quite comfortable. Next, he led me elsewhere. He kept the best for last. We went next door to Cartier, and then further back into a private room.

"Absolutely not," I told him when he showed me a piece of jewelry that had no price tag.

The pendulous earrings were white gold paved with diamonds. They had to be worth several times what the dress had cost.

"You will not argue with me on this. I've never bought this type of jewelry before for someone who wasn't my mother. Do me the courtesy of not saying no."

I was flabbergasted as he inserted them in my ears. I

wanted to run away screaming, this was too much. I was too shocked to react.

"All right, now can you show us a matching pendant?"

* * *

The house reeked of old money. It was a sprawling affair with a Mediterranean feel that had been built in the 1920s and renovated every decade. A large circular driveway was already filled with scores of luxury cars. Grayson told me about the gardens and the Olympic size swimming pool and the private beach but all I could see was the sheer size of it.

"Looks like we're late," I said.

"Never heard of the term fashionably late?"

"Yeah but not when it's your own party."

"It's not my party," he said as we got out of the car. "It's my father's party. I'm here because I help attract sycophants."

In the car, he'd told me how he had become one of the world's wealthiest men. The family had come to America two boats after the Mayflower and had made a fortune during the Industrial Revolution. A series of heirs had done their very best to squander it all over the years until Grayson's great-grandfather had put everything into trusts.

Barely into his teens, Grayson discovered his fondness for following the stock market. He impressed everyone in the family by quadrupling his allowance on a weekly basis. By the time he got to college, his family had given him control over a sizable amount of the fortune. He invested in a wide array of businesses and treated his portfolio like a hedge fund. He sheepishly admitted he was one of the few people who'd made out like a bandit with those toxic mortgage-backed securities.

Now he owned sizable chunks of some of the world's biggest companies. His own corporation was privately held despite the numerous appeals for him to go public. He said he liked to be in control. Somehow, I didn't doubt that for a minute.

The party was in full swing. There must have been 200

people and they all seemed to be dressed for the Oscars. A small orchestra provided lively music while waiters patrolled with trays filled with champagne glasses. This was a cut above the gatherings I was usually invited to at Ruby Tuesday.

"Come on, let me introduce you."

The next half-hour was dizzying. People all looked the same – middle-aged white folks with bling to spare – and they all had fancy WASP names like Harris Dundersfield Worthington IV and Elizabeth Longworth Donahough. I felt like Cinderella being taken to the country club.

He then took me to a specific couple which was obviously the center of attention. I promptly recognized them from the airport. They were his parents. My heart started to beat double its usual rate. Somehow, I didn't think giving a public hand job was exactly the appropriate prelude to meeting one's parents.

"Mom, dad, this is Merrin."

"Good evening," the parents said one after the other, shaking my hand.

"A pleasure to meet you, Senator and Mrs. Holmes."

"How exactly do you know my son, dear?" his mother asked.

"Well, it's one of those…"

I made your son cum in row 23 and then he bought me $50,000 worth of jewelry. I smiled politely but was starting to panic. Suddenly, I felt Grayson's hand rubbing my shoulder in comfort.

"I crossed Merrin's path recently and we hit it off. Mom, when she saw you earlier she didn't know who you were and she said to me you were beautiful."

"Oh, what a nice thing to say!"

"She was evidently made for politics," the Senator pitched in and everyone laughed. "What line of work are you in?"

I was pretty sure that being a secretary wasn't something highly regarded in these circles so I fudged the truth a little.

"I'm in the engineering business."

No one called me on it and I had a feeling that question was only asked out of politeness. Grayson soon took over the conversation and talked about the party. It was being held to raise money for the family foundation's poverty initiative but it was essentially a way to sway voters and eventual campaign supporters. Within moments, other people wanted a word with the Senator and Grayson led me away.

"The people who truly rule the country are in this room," he said into my ear. "You could start a war across the globe just by shaking the right hands."

"That's... disconcerting."

"Does that turn you on, Merrin?"

I looked up sharply at him. I knew some women got aroused from such power. Was I one of them? As we continued shaking guests' hands, I realized people were more deferential to Grayson than to his father. He wasn't the one in politics but he was the most powerful man in the room.

Without warning, I felt his hand travel from the small of my back down to my butt. He caressed it gently and I was positively shocked that he would do this in public. At least in the airplane we had been covered by a blanket.

CHAPTER 5

"Grayson, what are you doing?"

"I'm giving you what you want."

"You think I want to be fondled in the middle of your reception?"

"I know you do. Tell me," he whispered with his mouth close enough to my ear so that his breath made me shiver. "Can you feel the heat growing between your legs?"

His deep voice, the warmth of his breath, that's what was getting to me. His stroking hand was the cherry on the proverbial sundae. I looked at him with my lips parted. I wasn't even sure if I wanted him to stop or continuing. How could he have this effect on me? He grinned at my awkwardness.

"Come with me."

His hand returned to the small of my back and he led me away. We went around the grand staircase and stopped behind a row of potted ficus and cordyline plants. We were somewhat shielded from the party but anyone staring directly would be able to see us.

"What are you doing?" I asked again, certain that people would run out screaming if we were discovered.

"Can't you tell yet that I like you a lot?"

With a wicked smirk, he brought his face next to mine. I thought he was going to kiss me – at last! His lips brushed against my skin and he inhaled deeply. Instead of meeting my lips, he kissed my neck. I basked in the incredibly intimate feeling when I noticed he was doing this to divert my attention.

"Grayson!"

His right hand was between my legs and climbing. His strong fingers trailed up my smooth thigh. He stopped and rubbed circles against my creamy flesh. If this was all he had in mind I decided I could handle it. But no, it was only the beginning.

"Oh…"

He cupped my mound and let his middle finger dig into it. Unable to resist, I closed my eyes and exhaled loudly. How could he do this in public once again? How could I be so weak as to not push him away?

"You're not just hot down there, are you? You're wet too."

"Please, stop. We can't do this here."

"Why not? It's my party, I'm paying for all this. I can do what I want."

He caressed me with more vigor, making the fabric of my panties soak up my wetness. I wanted to hate this but I couldn't. I had flashbacks to our afternoon together, to the shameless things I'd done. It was so wrong but my body wanted more. I wanted more!

"Is that why you're doing this to me, Grayson? I'm the only person at this party who's not under your control?"

"No. You're the only person who's actually *enjoying* being under my control."

"Who says I'm enjoying this?"

All of a sudden, he pulled my underwear aside and inserted a finger into me. I gasped in shock. Mostly, I was overwhelmed by the instant pleasure he was offering me. This was the first time he touched me down there and his digit between my folds was so much better than I could ever have imagined.

"Any more lies you want to tell me, Merrin?"

He continued to caress me, coating his fingers with my arousal, and then he pulled back. Why did he keep denying me my release? I watched his glistening fingers and I was certain he would suck them into his mouth like he had done before. But no, this time he decided to be a cruel. He brought his hand up and wiped himself on my neck.

"What are you doing?"

"I want everyone to smell you. I want everybody to know how excited you are. Will you do that for me?"

The choice was clear, I should've told him no. I was about to when my voice caught in my throat. His suggestion – his order – made the heat flare between my legs.

"And to make things more interesting," he continued. "I want you to take your panties off."

This time I didn't offer a comment to translate my outrage. Besides, it was the second time today he'd talked me out of my unmentionables. In the great scheme of things, it was a step down from having his fingers inside of me and having my scent smeared around my neck. I was enthralled by his voice, by his eyes. I couldn't deny him anything. I was completely and utterly under his control.

I hiked up my dress after looking through the leaves to make sure no one was watching and I pushed down my black panties. I lowered the hem again and lifted my head high to show him I was completely unfazed. I wasn't but he didn't need to know that. I looked left and right for somewhere to put the underwear and that's when he snatched it away from me.

"Will you do me the honor of holding on to these?"

He brought the panties up to his face and he huffed conspicuously, all the while staring at me. Was he defying me? Was he hoping to get a rise out of me? In any case, he wouldn't get it. I was determined to call his bluff. I was determined not to show that this whole thing was exciting me. I was failing miserably.

He folded the underwear and pocketed it. Then, he gave me his elbow to escort me back into the fray. I took it and pretended I wasn't mortified. We walked through the crowd and he made a show of stopping at every cluster of guests.

"This is my friend Merrin. She's excited to be here."

He grinned at me mischievously and I don't know to this day how I refrained from slapping him. How could I do something so crazy? People had to smell my musky aroma! They all did a double take when they shook my hand but further than they didn't mention it.

Grayson led me to another group of people. The person at

the center of it was pushing 60 and the woman next to him —
his wife — seemed like the type who organized church bake
sales.

"Fred, how are you? Any word on lowering those pesky
interest rates?"

"You'll be the first to know, Grayson. As always."

"Merrin, I'd like you to meet the chairman of the Federal
Reserve and his lovely wife Grace. Word on Capitol Hill is that
they met at a swinger's party."

The comment was so ludicrous that Fred laughed
wholeheartedly. His wife took it differently. She choked on her
champagne.

"Here, let me help you."

The billionaire pulled out my panties. They were folded into
a perfect square, just like a handkerchief. He reached forward
and delicately wiped the woman's mouth. It was kind and
innocuous but there was no way she could miss the fragrance.
Her eyes grew as big as saucers. As quickly as he had come to
her aid, Grayson retreated.

"Don't worry, this happens all the time to women around
me. They can't seem to help themselves from getting wet."

He said that as a joke but the woman swiftly understood
and locked eyes with me. Her husband was oblivious and
started talking about finance. He had the most important man
in the room before him and he wasn't about to squander the
opportunity. The two men went into a quick discussion about
the acid test of the liquidity ratio of European markets through
the spectrum of asset turnover. Or something.

"Enjoy the rest of the evening," Grayson said. "I'll see you
later."

While we walked away, I couldn't stop thinking about my
damp underwear being shoved in the face of a highborn lady.
The whole thing had been so outrageous, I'd never done
something like this before. Death would have been preferable.
However, watching Grayson so poised, so in control of
everything around him made my heart lurch. I was becoming
another woman by his side.

A better woman.

"Why do you do these things to me?" I asked.

"Good things or bad things?"

"Good things but you're turning me into a bad girl."

"Took you long enough."

CHAPTER 6

I was more than ready and didn't even put up a fight when he wrangled me into the library. I didn't care that it wasn't a proper bedroom. I would have let him take me into a barn filled with rowdy animals if it meant I would finally get some relief. As soon as the door closed behind us, I threw my arms around his neck.

He looked into my eyes as if he was surprised by my sudden dominance. He was perhaps even a little proud. I didn't take the time to bask in my newfound position of power. I had other things on my mind. I had other pressing needs. I pulled him into my arms and kissed him hard and fast. I came to the realization this was our first real kiss. After all the teasing, after the decadent mile high masturbation and the public fingering, we were going back to basics.

My lips crushed against his and I was lost. Our mouths moved in harmony and I tasted him for the first time. Our tongues danced, fought against one another. We probed and explored each other and it was more intimate than anything we'd done so far. I never would have believed that it would turn out like this.

Holding me tight in embrace, he marched me back until I hit something. I instinctively reached behind me to feel against what I was standing. It was a table covered with soft felt. It was a pool table. I didn't have time to give it further thought because Grayson was kissing me anew. His hands were all over me as he delivered gentle pecks down my neck.

"Oh, Grayson…"

He touched me eagerly. His hands roamed over my chest, down my curves. He surveyed every inch of my ample cleavage

31

through the dress.

"Do you know the effect you have on me?"

While he said that, he grabbed my wrist and led me between his legs. I didn't need any additional prodding and hurriedly felt his crotch. The lump was sizable, inviting. It anything, it was bigger than it had been on the plane. It was scorching against my hand, so ready to do more than mere teasing. So I teased him some more.

"Don't you want this inside of you?" he asked.

I did, so much! However, he had tortured me all evening long and payback was delicious. I rubbed the area all around his groin, carefully avoiding touching his bulge directly. He breathed harder, almost moaning. I had to be doing something right.

"Are you getting back at me for this evening?"

I smiled. "I'm getting back at you for making me jack you off in the middle of a crowded airplane."

He grinned in return and quickly wrapped his arms around me. He pulled my body to his and kissed me fiercely. He pressed himself against me as if he wanted me to be a part of him. I ran my hands through his hair, unable to quench my thirst.

I was ready for more. I was ready for my reward. I saw in his eyes that he no longer wished to torment me. He was going to allow me to participate. He was going to allow me to reach Nirvana at last. I brought my hands down to his crotch again and fumbled with his belt. Once I had it unbuckled, I surprised myself at how skillful I was at undoing his pants.

"You arouse me so much, Merrin."

I witnessed this fact firsthand when I finally freed him. His member was long and engorged. Even though I had played with it to completion earlier, it was my first time seeing it in the flesh, so to speak. Its size was both mesmerizing and a little frightening. On the other hand, I couldn't wait to feel it, all of it. I had no doubt as to its charm.

I grasped it between my fingers and gave it a few playful tugs. Grayson exhaled loudly and pushed my hand away. He was too close, I could tell.

"No more messing around," he said.

He hiked up my dress and for once I accommodated him by spreading my legs. He touched me down there, finding me moister than I'd ever been. I moaned at his touch and that made him smile. I put my hand on his, intent on spurring him on, but he retreated.

With his pants around his ankles, he waddled forward and I knew what he wanted. I started breathing faster at what he was about to do. I leaned back further until I was essentially sitting on the edge of the pool table.

"Do it," I pleaded.

I opened my legs in invitation. I looked down as he grabbed his considerable length into his fist. He took great care of guiding himself between my folds, making me shudder at his caress. He found my entrance, glanced up at me, and rolled his hips.

"Oh God…"

He sank into me glorious inch by glorious inch. He was big and long but he seemingly was made for me. He sheathed himself completely, taking my breath away. At my reaction, he put his mouth on mine and kissed me languorously, making his tongue swirl around mine.

He started to pull out and I was afraid this had been nothing more than another big tease. But no, at the last minute he plunged back in. I cried plaintively into his mouth. His hands shot to my chest. He lowered the straps of my dress and freed my heavy breasts from the lacy bra.

"You're so beautiful," he whispered.

He caressed my flesh, finding all the sensitive spot. I was attacked by a series of tremors and I had no idea which stimulation was causing them. My body acting of its own accord, I lied back on the table. He didn't object and instantly I knew why. This new angle offered deeper penetration.

"Feels so good, Grayson."

The compliment gave him strength, he picked up the pace. He was ravaging me, taking me so shamelessly in ways I had only dreamed of. I was at his mercy, ravenous for his body, for all the pleasure he could provide.

I let my own hands wander across my curves, touching myself openly. Everything I touched became scorching in seconds. The secret sweetness down below was spreading like a wildfire.

"More," I wailed. "Give me more!"

As I said that, I started to lose my senses. My thoughts became incoherent, my vision was blurred. All I could focus on it was Grayson moving within me, his shaft plowing through my channel, stoking my desire.

His grunting became louder, hungrier. I felt his fire flaring within me. He wouldn't last long, nor could he. This suited me just fine. I was myself aching for relief. I was on the brink of tumbling into the orgasmic abyss.

"Right there, Grayson…"

I didn't have to say anymore. He kneaded my chest with renewed vigor and accelerated his thrusting. His hard steel hit all the right notes and at once my body began to tingle. There were goose bumps all over my skin and electric currents shot through me.

"Oooohh," I cried, the voice catching in my throat.

The world went blank as the pleasure crescendoed. I saw colors, beautiful colors dancing through my tightly shut eyes. My climax was a long time coming and I welcomed it with open arms. I arched my back, digging into the pool table as much as I could. I had no defense against the blissful onslaught.

"Get ready," he snarled breathlessly.

At the same time, he swelled inside of me. He was so big, filling me so well! He rolled his hips a few more times and then he erupted deep into my womb.

"Aaarrgghhh…"

His frothy seed was sizzling and it reignited my fire. He came and came again. His tumescence continued to sway back and forth within me as he emptied himself. Grayson leaned forward and crushed his lips against mine. He kissed me tenderly as we both rode out our dreamlike ecstasy.

I hugged him firmly as if I was afraid someone would steal him away from me. This was so crazy, it had happened so fast, that I wasn't completely certain of even being awake. After the longest time, we both stopped thrashing, both stopped panting. We simply stared at each other.

"Thank you," I whispered.

"You don't have to thank me for anything. Not ever."

"You say that like you plan on seeing me again."

"Would you have something against that?"

I stared into his eyes to see whether or not he was being serious. In my experience, men said all sorts of nice things before making love with you. But afterwards was another story. They usually slept and left, oftentimes the other way around. Was why Grayson so different?

"I'd prefer you told me right now what your intentions are. I've had my fair share of disappointments and I'm not good with them. So if you're trying to be nice just so you can brush me off tomorrow, I'd rather you let me down right now."

"I can't see the future, Merrin. However, I can tell you that I'm being honest with you. I like you, I want to see you again. You wouldn't believe how many times I've been slapped for trying to finger a girlfriend in public."

I actually gasped at that. He did that with everyone?

"So you like me because I'm docile?"

That made him grin. "I like you because I could see you enjoy these games as much as I do."

I opened my mouth to protest but I could only manage a stammer. I didn't want to enjoy what he did to me. It was perverse, so contrary to whom I really was. Yet, I couldn't deny what a thrill it had been to do all these things, to obey his commands. It was all so unlike me that I'd never expected to feel this way.

"I don't know if I can ever do that again, Grayson. It was wild, it was fun, but it's not me."

"It is you. Do you know how I know? Because you didn't push me away. This *is* you and it's only the beginning."

Even though he was softening, he was still inside of me. I involuntarily quivered around him and he smirked knowingly. My body was betraying me!

"Come on, let's go back to the party. I want to see their nostrils flare as they smell what we've done. That will get you ready for round two."

"I... I can't. I have to go back to my grandmother."

"I think she'll understand you have urges. I intend to take care of those urges. Have you ever done it on a beach in Thailand? I have business there next week. I want you with me."

"My grandmother, she needs me."

"I need you, Merrin."

As he kissed me, I knew right then that I was his. I would never be complete without his subtle power. It made me stronger. It made us whole.

*****

THE POWER BILLIONAIRE 2: DOMINATED CURVES AND DESIRE

CHAPTER 1

"Relax," Grandma Edna said from the kitchen. "He's gonna call."

"Maybe I should leave him a message. Maybe he forgot my number. Maybe he lost his phone, had to get a new one, and lost my information in the process."

This was a frighteningly real possibility. How could he get in touch with me if he didn't have my number anymore? I was about to call his office in New York to tell his assistant where I was and how Grayson could reach me when my grandmother gave me the evil eye.

"Don't be acting stupid on me, Merrin. I ever told you about Mrs. Heptinstall who lives on the third floor? Small woman, big hair, very unfortunate. She looks like one of them cadavers on *CSI*, you know, when they show them after the autopsy. Same skin tone."

"What about her, Grandma?" I asked as I joined her at the counter.

"Mrs. Heptinstall, she used to have a man. Paraded him everywhere like some award-winning schnauzer. Mostly she kept him on a leash, had all of them activities planned out. They went on dates all the time. The mixer at the VFW, strip bingo —"

"Strip bingo?"

"I hear it's all the rage what with all them hippies being senior citizens nowadays. Marshall Stefkovich keeps bugging me to go. I'm still thinking it over."

"Grandma, please. I don't need to know about these things."

I was about to retch as I pictured a room full of wrinkly old people getting naked in front of their bingo cards.

"I'm trying to lose a few pounds before committing to the idea. Might be swell to see Herb Blaskey in the buff. He used to be a fireman, you know. Forty years ago. Anyway, Mrs. Heptinstall kept calling her man all the time. She called him before breakfast, she called him *after* breakfast, at night, on weekends. After a while he stopped picking up."

"I'm assuming you have a big shiny point, Grandma?"

"He had another woman," she said, glancing at me like this was the most profound secret ever shared.

"So what are you saying? You think Grayson has already forgotten about me and that he has another woman in his life? Already?"

"Sometimes Merrin, it's better to be prepared for bad news, all I'm saying."

She put her leftovers in the fridge, turned to me with a surprisingly sweet and understanding smile, and gave me a quick hug. I kissed the top of her head and watched her disappear into the living room where she was no doubt in a hurry to catch up on her shows.

At the same time, I couldn't shake her words. Could Grayson have another woman in his life? My heart was screaming that it was impossible, not after all we'd been through in the last few weeks. And yet, I couldn't dismiss the idea on an intellectual level. Grayson Holmes was one of the wealthiest men in the world. He was handsome, popular, smart, and extremely powerful. How could he be satisfied with someone like me? I was nothing but a chubby secretary.

We had met on a plane and our attraction had been almost instantaneous. His commanding voice had done me in. I'd had no choice but to follow his prompts, his devious orders which had led us to masturbate each other right there in public. It had been impossible to resist him.

I was certain I'd never see him again once we landed but he invited me to a glamorous party at his family estate in Palm Beach. He bought me designer clothes and the kind of jewelry that could refinance an entire neighborhood. How could I not fall for him? How could I not let him take me on the pool table in that fancy library?

Again, I was expecting this to the end of it. Be grateful for the good moments, the small blessings, that was my motto. But no, there was more. He had business in Thailand and begged me to come with him. Grandma Edna said she would strike me from her will if I didn't go. I was spending time with her in Boca Raton while she recuperated from her gallbladder surgery so I felt a little guilty about it. When I still wasn't sure, she winked at me and gave me some birth control pills. I didn't even want to contemplate what she was doing with those.

We flew to Bangkok on Grayson's private jet. It was outfitted with a lounge and bedroom and we took advantage of it for more than sleeping. There's something to be said about the benefits of turbulence when a fine-looking man is lying on top of you. I saw all kinds of stars that night.

We stayed at the Sukhothai Hotel, in the top floor suite. I'd never seen such luxury. It was huge, over 2,000 square feet. It was twice as big as my apartment in New York City and the view of the lavish gardens down below was breathtaking.

Before we had even settled in, he took me against the grand piano. I was bent over it with my skirt hiked up around my waist and I didn't even flinch when he pulled my hair back as he entered me. It was fast and animalistic, utterly fulfilling. I wanted for this to last forever as I was still not getting used to his sudden needs. However, just the opportunity to please him excited me.

For the next three days, I was mostly on my own. We had passionate encounters when we were together on mornings and nights but then he would disappear for strings of meetings with various business tycoons. To make up for it, we then flew down to Phuket. When I saw the word on his tablet I revealed how unworldly I was by thinking it was pronounced Fuck-It. This amused him greatly for the whole trip. Needless to say, it took me five seconds to learn how to properly say Pooh-ket.

The heat was almost overwhelming. It was humid and sunny and the resort town was built like paradise. I promptly forgot about the heat when we got to the Banyan Tree. The hotel was essentially a collection of villas, each more luxurious than the next. Unsurprisingly, Grayson had booked the best and the largest for us.

We had our own private pool and jacuzzi and I discovered the joys of being mounted while in the water. He couldn't be as rough and energetic as usual but he made up for it by pulling my hair again and pinching me in places I never knew would make me feel pleasure. My nipples were insanely sensitive afterwards but it was worth it.

So worth it...

We stayed in Phuket for another three fun-filled days and then it was time to head back to Florida where he dropped me off before continuing on to New York. He said he would call when he landed. That was two days ago.

"Merrin, are you still waiting next to the phone?"

"No, of course not!"

Technically, the phone was in my pocket so I wasn't next to it, more like on top of it. I charged it every four hours to make sure it was working and I checked my messages every 30 minutes. I even went to my profile on the phone company website to see if they had canceled my service for some reason. I was disappointed that it wasn't the case. Now I had no logical explanation as to why Grayson wasn't calling.

That wasn't true and I knew it. Occam's Razor dictated that the simplest explanation tended to be the correct one and I couldn't dismiss it. Grayson just wasn't into me. God, I sounded like some second rate self-help book! To make the pill easier to swallow, I decided that perhaps I had dreamed the whole experience after all.

"Come join me! The doctor is about to be voted off. I never liked him, way too smug. I don't trust men with so much hair. Have you seen his chest? I think birds are nesting in there. I wish they should dismember him instead."

"Grandma, you're awful and twisted. I love you so much."

I sat on the couch with my eyes riveted to the TV. I saw a blur of images but couldn't focus. All I was thinking about was what a fool I'd been thinking Grayson had actually liked me. Maybe a clean break like this was for the best. I decided I would send the jewelry to his Florida estate the next day. I was a lot of things but I wasn't a gold digger.

All of a sudden, the strident shriek of my grandmother's ancient phone resounded.

My heart started to beat a mile a minute. I'd been so stupid for doubting him. I got up to answer but my grandmother beat me to it.

"Hello?"

"Yes, she's here. Are you the beefcake?"

I snatched the phone away from her so fast that I was one flux capacitor short of traveling through time.

"Grayson?!"

"Merrin Rexford?"

The voice was nothing like Grayson's. It was deeper and had Southern inflections.

"Yes," I answered suspiciously.

"My name is James Evartt. We need to meet. I'm with Homeland Security."

CHAPTER 2

At first the man wanted to come over to my grandmother's unit. As convenient as it was, the words *Homeland Security* scared me. I was afraid something creepy and inappropriate would be said and I didn't want Grandma Edna to overhear. I loved her to death but I was certain I would become gossip fodder for months on end. So I agreed to meet him at a Denny's nearby.

For some reason he recognized me when I walked in and called me over to his booth. I understood that he probably had pulled my file from somewhere and studied my photograph. These days, everybody was on file somewhere. The moment I sat down, the waitress came over. Since this was the middle of the afternoon, we both ordered coffee only. When the waitress walked away, he flashed his credentials and we introduced each other.

"I'm glad you could meet me, Ms. Rexford."

"Sure. You said it was important."

"It is, believe me."

"And you said this is about Grayson Holmes?"

I tried to make my voice steady as I said that but I wasn't certain I succeeded.

"Why don't we start with the beginning? How did you come to meet him?"

"We were seated together on a plane from New York."

As he took notes, I told him how his private jet had been unavailable and he was forced to fly commercial. I omitted the details of how he had talked me into touching the hardness between his legs, under the blanket.

"We became friends, I guess. That night, he invited me to a

party at his house in Palm Beach. It was packed with rich people, politicians, not really my crowd. But he made me feel so welcome. Grayson is good at that."

"And then the two of you went to Thailand together."

It wasn't a question. I even had a feeling he already knew about everything I'd told him so far. His eyes were hard, difficult to read. It was as if he was defying me and yet was amused by my responses.

The waitress came back with our coffee and I took the opportunity to watch him as he declined milk and sugar. He wasn't as tall as Grayson but he was bulkier. Just from his neck I knew he spent a lot of time at the gym. He was probably the type to take part in amateur bodybuilding competitions. He had a chiseled face, all angles and none of them were displeasing. All in all, he was top-tier material.

"Special Agent Evartt, why am I here?"

"We're having a chat."

"I'm wondering why. You seem to know everything already."

"I'm interested in Thailand."

"You should go sometime, beautiful country."

He grinned and sipped coffee.

"You went to Bangkok, spent three days in one of the most expensive hotels in Southeast Asia."

"Grayson is one of the wealthiest persons in the world."

Evartt nodded. "Is that why you like him?"

"What kind of question is that? What kind of person do you think I am?"

"You tell me."

I stared at him, seething, and he stared right back. The hint of a smirk was growing across his lips.

"I don't have to put up with this crap," I muttered as I began to climb to my feet.

He put his warm hand on mine and I stopped, more shocked than anything.

"I'm sorry I implied anything that made you seem unladylike. I apologize."

He was sincere and I sat back down. "Why don't you get to your important questions?"

"Fair enough," he said after a moment. "In Thailand, were you with Mr. Holmes at all times?"

"No, of course not."

"On how many occasions were the two of you apart?"

"Well, when we went to Phuket we were pretty much always together. Before that, during those three days in Bangkok, that was for his business. Between breakfast and lunch and between lunch and dinner he was away doing billionaire stuff."

"Such as?"

"He didn't tell me the details and I never asked."

"Weren't you curious about it?"

I shrugged as I played with my coffee. "He said he was meeting people. What difference does it make if he's discussing the transition of scalable paradigms or incubating bricks-and-clicks convergence?"

"You seem to know the lingo."

"I hear it all the time at my job. Most of it is just a way for executives to justify the hundred grand they spent on their useless education. The words don't mean anything. This is another reason I didn't ask Grayson about the details of his meetings."

"So you never saw who he was meeting with?"

"No."

"If I showed you pictures, you wouldn't be able to tell me if you've seen them?"

"The only people I saw, Special Agent Evartt, were the hotel staff and restaurant waiters. I don't know anything about anything."

"Merrin, you're not saying this to protect him, are you?"

"Protect him from what?" I blurted out, not even realizing we were now on a first-name basis. I leaned forward across the table. "Why are you questioning me about him? Why is Homeland Security interested in Grayson Holmes?"

He stared at me with those mysterious eyes for long

seconds before standing up. As he reached into his pocket to get a business card, his charcoal suit opened up. I not only saw his ominous sidearm but I also realized I was correct about him being muscular. His white shirt clung to him in such a way that I couldn't avert my gaze.

"If you learn anything, if you suddenly decide to talk, give me a call, all right?"

He handed me the business card and our fingers made contact. My breath caught in my throat. I hadn't felt like that since first meeting Grayson.

* * *

I was actually shaking when I got back to my grandmother's apartment. In hindsight, the questions had been innocuous. But why was Homeland Security interested in Grayson in the first place? Had he done something wrong? Did he know something that could hurt the government somehow?

What if this was some sort of ploy from a competitor? I'd read enough books to know that deception was often at the heart of corporate shenanigans.

Fortunately, Grandma Edna wasn't home when I got there. She left a note saying she was meeting Mrs. Allendorf for, her exact words, *a demonstration on waxing our Brazilian.* At least I wouldn't have to explain anything to her. And I needed to think. What should I do?

Should I completely forget about Grayson? After all, if he was involved in anything shady it would be wiser for me to stay away. Then again, what if it really was a set-up from one of his enemies? Shouldn't I warn him?

I settled on Option B. It would give me a genuine reason to call him without appearing needy. As much as I told myself it was strictly business, there was no suffocating the butterflies in my stomach. I sat down at the kitchen table and dialed his number using my grandmother's phone since she had a nationwide long distance plan.

What if I got his voicemail? I started to panic and silently went through a casual-but-serious version of what I would say. It kept ringing.

"Yes?"

It was his voice! My heart lurched. It was incredible how I missed hearing it. I never would've believed our short time together would have affected me so much.

"Hello? Anyone there?"

"Uh, hi! Grayson, it's good to hear from you."

What had I just said? *Doofus!*

"Who is this?"

"It's me, Merrin."

"Oh, what's the matter?"

That's it? No *how are you, I'm happy to speak to you,* or *I apologize for being such an insensitive jerk and didn't call you for two days after all the sex we've had?* I was bristling.

"I'm sorry," he continued with a softer tone. "I didn't mean it like that. How are you, Merrin?"

"Uh, I'm good. I'm having a lot of fun with my grandmother," I lied. "Right now we're playing this card game she learned at the senior center. It involves putting teaspoons between your toes. It's a lot of fun."

I considered covering the mouth piece and yelling something to my imaginary grandmother but decided it was probably too much.

"Sounds like you're having a blast. I wanted to call you but it's been pretty hectic around here. As soon as the plane touched down in New York we've been in kind of a crisis mode regarding some contracts, or lack thereof, in Azerbaijan. Every time I have a second to myself I fall asleep."

"Oh, I'm sorry. I shouldn't have called."

"No, no, it's fine now. Was there something specific on your mind or..." He lowered his voice. "Or did you want me to tell you how sexy you are? I bet I could make you play with yourself right now for me. Did you ever have phone sex?"

At the mention of this, at hearing his honey-dipped voice, my defenses crumbled. I remembered all the things we'd done together. I pictured his throbbing erection in my hand, his thrusting between my legs. I recalled all the sensations he gave me in such a limited timeframe. Flashes of heat spread through my abdomen and my breath came out in spurts.

"Grayson, no. I have to talk to you."

"You sure I can't talk to you into using your fingers to caress yourself for me? I love hearing you when you come."

I closed my eyes and shook my head. I couldn't let him get the upper hand.

"This is important. A man came to see me today."

"Hmmm, and did he do things to you? Did you enjoy what he did?"

"Stop it, I'm serious. He said his name is James Evartt and he's from Homeland Security. His credentials looked legit."

"What did he want?"

His voice was back to normal, strong and professional.

"He asked questions about our trip to Thailand, especially Bangkok. He wanted to know what you were doing, who you met with."

"I see. And what did you tell him?"

"Nothing. There was nothing to tell. We were together only at the hotels so I didn't see anyone."

"Right. It's probably nothing."

"Is this real, Grayson? Is this a for-real federal agent asking questions about you?"

"What do you mean, *a for-real federal agent?*"

"Well, I thought maybe it should be one of your competitors. You know, a gambit to make you – or me – spill the beans on some secret deal you're working on."

That made him laugh good-naturedly. "I think you've read too many books and seen too many movies. And to answer your question, yes, that's probably a for-real federal agent. Impersonating federal personnel carries such a penalty – we're talking prison here – that nobody's done that since the 90s."

I nodded emphatically as if he was in the same room with me. I wished he was.

"So you're sure it's nothing then?"

"Well, on second thought, maybe it would be better to find

out."

"Are you gonna put one of your security people on it?"

"I have a better idea. The federal agent would just see right through my people. However, there's one person he would never suspect."

"Who?"

"You, Merrin."

"You're kidding me, right?" I said with my mouth hanging open.

"I don't just want you to question him. I want you to finesse all you can out of him."

"I can't do that, I can barely finesse myself into a pair of pants."

He snorted back a chuckle. "Give yourself more credit. It'll be easy. You go to him and you flirt."

"Yeah, like that's gonna work. Besides, I can't just flip on a switch and suddenly be some sophisticated femme fatale."

I thought about how I looked. I was plus-size and so outside what the average femme fatale looked like.

"Merrin, you have no idea how much power you yield. You don't have to be anyone else, you just need to be yourself. Your eyes, your mouth, your magnificent curves, let them work in your favor. Seduce the information out of him."

"That will never work."

"Wear the necklace I gave you and use your charms to ease into that conversation."

I shrugged. *I'll play along*, I thought. *I'll pretend I can actually do these things.*

"But what if he wants more than just a conversation?"

"Are you willing to do anything to reach your goal, Merrin?"

"Yeah but..."

"But what? Are you willing to do anything to help *me*?"

"What if... What if it actually turns into a situation where... my seduction works? What if... What if he wants to have sex?"

"Do it."

CHAPTER 3

I was shocked. I didn't realize the phone was no longer clutched to my ear.

"Merrin? Merrin, are you there?"

"You want me to have sex with another man?" I finally said.

"You've seen him, right? You've seen this Evartt guy? Is he an old person?"

"No, in his 30s."

"Is he repulsive?"

"No," I replied as I pictured the federal agent. He was the opposite of repulsive. He was yummilicious.

"Then there's no problem, is there?"

"There's us. Is there an us?"

"I like to think that there is. I like you very much, Merrin. You know that. If you mean, am I happy to share you with another man? The answer is no. But am I willing to do that? Absolutely. If you do that for me, if you're willing to go that extra mile, I would forever be grateful."

"I don't know..."

I thought of the expensive jewelry he'd given me, of the once-in-a-lifetime trip to Asia. Didn't I owe him? On the other hand, thinking along those terms made me feel bad. It made me feel cheap, like a prostitute. Yet, at my very core I wanted to return the kindness he had shown me.

"Most people would be delighted to be encouraged to sleep with someone else," he said. "You're getting a free pass."

"But still."

"Anyway, I think we're getting ahead of ourselves. I'm not sending you a buck naked to his bed. You're just going to start a conversation. If you make him talk, the whole debate becomes moot."

Grayson was right, of course. My fears were all hypothetical. He would most likely not be interested in me even if I jumped him with a pork chop around my neck. The worst that would happen was that he would see right through me and brush me off.

"Okay, I'll do it."

* * *

The business card was unnecessary in contacting Special Agent James Evartt. Grayson had a much more devious approach. Once he was certain I would go to in this, we hung up and I went to take a bite to eat and a shower. An hour later, I was dressed to the nines and Grayson called me back. He told me what hotel the federal agent was staying at in Fort Lauderdale. I was impressed. It was useful to have a father who was a U.S. Senator.

I took a taxi south and in less than a half-hour I was dropped off at the hotel. It wasn't located on the beach – or even on the Intracoastal, for that matter. It was a mid-range establishment, clean and probably rather affordable. Evartt wouldn't be criticized for being a big spender.

The most important thing Grayson told me when he called me back was the agent's precise location. He actually had GPS coordinates of where he was standing in real-time. This was spooky and I wondered how he'd even gotten such information. The billionaire didn't call me back while I was in the cab which told me the man was still at the same position.

I walked into the hotel and headed left toward the restaurant. Scanning the unimpressive crowd, it was easy to spot Evartt. He was sitting at the bar nursing a colorful concoction and toying with his iPad. I took a deep breath, remembered what I was going to say, and marched forward. My new Louboutin heels made me taller and somehow made me feel more confident. I kept my head high and pretended I was Lauren Bacall.

"Well, that's a surprise!" I said as I sat next to him and feigned being taken aback by him.

His first instinct was to frown. I knew right away he was a seasoned federal agent. He didn't take well to coincidences.

"Ms. Rexford, what are you doing here?"

"I could ask you the same thing."

"I'm staying here, this is my hotel."

"Really? Small world! I'm meeting a friend here. She's in town for the pharmaceutical conference."

This was another piece of information Grayson had given me. There was indeed a convention of Pfizer employees at this hotel.

"Oh," he said. "I reckoned perhaps you'd come here to talk to me again. Maybe you decided to do the right thing, decided to talk."

"Sorry, I already said everything I knew. Say, what are you drinking?"

"Pink daiquiri."

"Sounds delicious."

I waved at the bartender and ordered one for myself.

"Put it on my tab," Evartt said.

"Thank you, that's so nice! So you're not located in South Florida?"

"What makes you say that?"

"We're meeting at a hotel, aren't we?"

"Maybe I live nearby. Maybe I just like the way he prepares pink daiquiris."

That gave me pause. I was about to concede the point when I noticed for all its wonder, his skin was too pale for a Florida resident.

"No, you were raised somewhere in the South but you live in a cooler place now."

"Good observation. You should be one of us."

I beamed as I watched the barman mix together white rum, maraschino liqueur, lemon juice, simple syrup, and grapefruit juice. He vigorously shook the stainless steel mixer and then strained the drink into a martini glass.

"To getting a tan," Evartt said, raising his glass.

"To getting a tan."

We drank and I used the silence to think about my next move. How could I go about making him talk?

"So, will you be returning home soon?"

"I was thinking about finishing this drink first."

"I meant..."

"I know what you meant," he answered with a smirk. "I just love how bold you are. It's like you're fishing for walleye with dynamite."

"I'm not sure what you're talking about, Special Agent Evartt."

I took a sip to cover my nervousness. It was already falling apart. I knew I wasn't gifted with this sort of thing.

"Call me James."

"All right, James. But that doesn't change the fact that I'm only making conversation."

"Sure. You know who else approaches strangers in bars like this to make conversation?"

"No, who?"

"Escorts."

I was so stunned by his reply that I straightened up and turned sideways to face him. "Excuse me? Did you just accuse me of being a prostitute?"

"I didn't accuse you of anything. I'm just stating a fact. It ain't my problem if you're feeling threatened."

"I just came here to have a good time and you being rude is really ruining it, James."

I turned further so I could get up from the stool but he put a hand on my forearm, stopping me cold.

"Wait, I apologize."

"You're sorry you called me a whore?"

"I apologize you won't be finishing your drink. The last sip of a pink daiquiri is always the best."

He accompanied the statement with a disarming smile. He was so handsome even though he was virtually mocking me.

The Hawaiian shirt he was wearing had trouble hiding his muscles and the buttons were straining against his chest. He was definitely the bad boy I never would've expected to talk to me back in high school.

"Fine but I'm not forgiving you. You're on probation."

"Now you're talking my language."

We drank some more and I wondered if I should've walked away. Was it suspicious that I stayed here even though he'd accused me of being a prostitute? Wouldn't someone with no agenda just stomp away? In the end I decided they wouldn't. Evartt had that look in his eyes, that predatory glare which was impossible to resist. He reminded me of Grayson but in a much more feral manner.

"So," he continued. "What did your boyfriend said to convince you to interrogate me?"

Oh shit!

"Uh, I… You're imagining things."

"Am I? I don't believe in coincidences. I think Mr. Moneybags sent you over to find out more about me."

"That's ridiculous," I spat as I shook my head.

"The question I'm asking myself is, what kind of a sick bastard sends his woman into the lion's den?" He leaned toward me. "What kind of instructions did he give you? Did he ask you to seduce me?"

"You're disgusting."

"You know I'm trained to find out when people are lying to me. You don't find me disgusting at all. Your nostrils are flaring, you're blinking faster, your pupils are dilated. You're getting aroused, sweetheart."

How could he know these things? I was doing my best to think about innocuous things like badminton and unicorns. I was trying hard to deny that he was one of the most dangerous-looking men I'd ever met.

How could he know that heat was spreading between my legs?

"You… You don't know anything about me, James."

"I know you want me, Merrin. And you know what else?"

He brought his face an inch away from my ear. "Even though I could lose my job over this, I want you too."

I stopped breathing. Could I really go through with this? Would it help Grayson in the long-run?

CHAPTER 4

I was breathing quickly when we entered his room. He flipped on the light and I was surprised at how tidy everything was. There were no clothes strewn about, no newspapers or candy wrappers littering the floor. I stood straight and wiped my moist hands on my hips while he locked the door.

This is it. I'm really doing this.

Without warning, his hand was on my shoulder. He brushed his fingers down on my bare skin and it sent shivers up and down my spine. Before I could decide what to do, I felt his breath on my neck. He lowered his head and kissed my shoulder before moving closer, nuzzling my neck.

"Oh God…"

He continued to kiss my soft flesh and made his way up to my ear which he started nibbling on. He blew warm air into it and it made my eyes roll back. I nearly lost my balance. At the same time, he caressed me with both hands, running his fingers up and down my arms and over my stomach.

This last part brought me back to reality. I wasn't a big fan of men touching me there as it only reminded me how I utterly differed from the girls in magazines. I spun on my heels and faced him. He grinned lazily, making me think of a cowboy.

"Come here, gorgeous."

He pulled me to him and planted his mouth on mine. His lips parted and he kissed me hungrily. His tongue was eager, unrelentingly probing my mouth until I had no choice but to return the favor. His kiss was demanding and I gave myself to it. I felt serenity wash over me and I wrapped my arms around his neck, pulling myself closer.

His hands were all over me and before long I was grinding

against him. I cursed my dress which was too tight to spread my legs like I wanted to. I forgot about trying to make him talk. I was the one who actually wanted to bring things to the next level. I had a need, a pressing need!

At last, we pulled apart to catch our breath. He looked at me, his eyes smoldering. It lips were slightly opened and he covertly licked them. It made my heart melt. He came to me again and I was getting ready for another make out session when he changed course. He nuzzled my neck again but this time it wasn't the main attraction. No, what he was actually focusing on was unzipping my dress.

This was real, there was no backing down now. He brought the zipper all the way down and then didn't waste a moment peeling my dress away from me. I was nervous, and wished the room was darker. Sadly, the bedside lamp was powerful and only offered mediocre shadows. He pushed the straps off my shoulders and let the dress pool around my ankles.

"You're beautiful," he said.

"You don't need to lie. I'm already in your room."

"You're right, you're not beautiful. You're stunning."

At least I wasn't actually naked. I was wearing a pink teddy with built-in cups which gave me the mother of all cleavages. It also worked well to hide my tummy. Then I remembered I was still wearing my pumps. Men usually reacted favorably to a half-naked woman in high heels.

He continued to stare at me and as he did so he unbuttoned his shirt. It was now my turn to lick my lips as I glimpsed his muscular body. Sure enough, when he tossed the shirt away, my mind was blown. His chest was made to study anatomy. I could see every muscle as it caught the light. His washboard abs alone would make nuns drool.

He came to me and his hands took me by surprise. I thought he was going to massage my full breasts but instead he pulled them out of the cups. They hung out pendulously, boldly on display. He ran his thumbs over the areolas until my nipple hardened. Then, he took a step back as if he wanted to admire his handiwork.

"It ain't the only thing that's getting stiff."

"I bet."

His crude language didn't offend me. I was far too involved for that.

"I want you to get on your knees and make your way over to me."

"Oh, okay," I said as I walked forward.

"No, stop. I said get on your knees and then come to me. I wanna see you crawl."

Puzzled at his request, I fell to my knees. I was actually relieved to get off my feet. For all their prettiness, these shoes were hell to wear. I waddled as best as I could until I got to him.

"Now touch it. See how you've made it."

I put both hands on his knees and slowly slid up toward his groin. I felt a bulge way sooner than I would've thought. The idea of touching it, of eventually seeing it, made heat flare between my legs. I could scarcely believe how my body reacted. This wasn't me, I was supposed to be a good girl.

It was my turn to lick my lips as I made contact with the lump between his legs. I didn't realize I'd stopped breathing until I ran out of air. I almost panted as I traced his sizable hardness with my fingers.

"Get it out."

He removed his gun and holster from his belt and put it on the dresser next to us. He was all about big guns, I saw. I undid his pants and let them drop. He was wearing briefs which made his erection even more prominent. I touched it again and felt it throb through the thin cotton. He exhaled audibly under my fingers.

"Release it. I want you to take it into your mouth."

I looked up at him quickly. This wasn't something I usually liked. Even Grayson never submitted me to this. Trying to hide my hesitancy, I pushed his underwear down. His shaft sprung up, making me think of a Jack-in-the-Box. It was shorter than I would've imagined but much, much thicker.

"In your mouth, I said."

Steeling my resolve, I took him in my hand and brought my head closer. His flesh was scorching. I felt his heart beat just by holding his length. It was beating fast. I tentatively licked the tip before taking the head between my lips. It wasn't bad. In fact, I was warming up to the idea. My body was definitely warming up.

"Take it, all of it."

I started to comply but I guess I wasn't going fast enough for him. He placed a hand behind my head and pushed me down. I almost gagged but his dominance was arousing. I never thought about resisting. There was also the fact that he felt good inside my mouth. His rod was pulsating in tandem with my movements.

"Yeah, pretend you're a good little whore. Take me deep."

He grabbed a handful of my hair and made me bob on him. I let my hands wander along his strong thighs, to his firm buttocks which I squeezed lightly. He didn't stop me so I did it again. All the while, I let him guide my movements. I used my tongue to give him extra pressure. He groaned in response so I knew I was doing something right.

All of a sudden, he yanked my head off him. He grabbed his shaft and slapped my face noisily with it. It was odd but strangely arousing. It was as if he was beating me into submission. And yet, it made me want to please him more. Me, Merrin Rexford who never was into oral sex, I was beginning to crave it.

I craned my neck to take him between my lips again but he backed away. I found myself pouting like a child who had just been denied a second lollipop.

"Now we see if acting like a whore is as exciting for you."

He pulled me to my feet and I took the opportunity to slip out of my shoes. He led me to the bed and pushed me down on it. The fact that the covers weren't turned down was a bit odd, like we were doing something illicit. He directed me to the middle of the mattress and got between my legs.

"You're overdressed."

With that, he grabbed the waistband of my panties and

pulled them off. Technically, my teddy covered most of my body save for my breasts – it even hung low enough to hide my womanhood – but I felt naked. I felt completely exposed. I pressed my legs together but he shook his head.

"Don't play coy with me now."

Grabbing my ankles, he forced my legs open. His eyes were riveted to my apex. He was smiling faintly.

"Is it as wet as it seems?"

Before I could answer, his hand was on me. He started by caressing the inside of my wide thighs, stroking the creamy flesh. He slowly made his way up and within seconds his fingers were on me. He delved between my folds and I had no choice but to purr.

"Oh yes, you are positively drenched. Was it taking me in your mouth or the fact that I was pushing down on your head? Or maybe you like looking at my body, uh? Some women can't get enough of it."

He might have something there, I thought. He was starting to sweat from our activities and it made him look like some wrestler from ancient Greece, all shiny and oozing sex appeal.

He lied down prone between my legs and I readily felt his breath over my damp quim. He flipped up the hem of my teddy which made my anxiety return. I sucked in my tummy in response. If he saw anything, if he didn't like what he witnessed, he didn't say a word. Instead, he brought his face lower still and made contact with me.

"Aaarrggh…"

His tongue lashes grew in speed and intensity. It didn't take long for the pressure to build up in my abdomen. I was fluttering all over, lost to his assault. I wasn't quite there yet but the sensation was incredible.

"Yes," I moaned. "Deeper."

He laved me with great care, using his entire mouth on my lush mound to stimulate every nerve ending. I was soaked from excitement and when I couldn't take it anymore it was my turn to put a hand behind his head and force him to finish me off.

He pushed my hand away and lifted his head. "You don't mess with this, y'hear?"

"But I'm so close."

I unconsciously gyrated my hips to make him see how much I needed this. No dice, he continued to stare at me.

"If you don't behave I'll be forced to tie you up. Don't make me do this, you slut."

His language shocked me and I nodded. He kept his eyes on me for a few more seconds and then dipped his head. He munched on me as if he was ravenous and I arched my back.

"Feels so good, James..."

Whenever I was close, he backed off and concentrated on a different part of my channel. One minute he had his fingers in me and the next he was kissing the inside of my thighs. It was as if he knew exactly how I felt and wanted to make me agonize.

"Please, just a little more!"

And then he entirely stopped. He got on his knees and I looked at him. My eyes fell to his midsection. He was harder than ever, standing at attention and ready for the main event. *Good*, I thought. I was ready too. I was desperate for him.

"You want this, uh? You want it?"

I nodded much more heartily than intended. "Yes, please."

"Okay, but you'll get it under my terms. I want you from behind."

I was secretly glad. I recalled all the times Grayson had taken me in this fashion. It never failed to be amazing. I quickly rose and got onto my hands and knees.

"I didn't say that's how I wanted you."

"But..."

Before I could protest further, he pushed me so I was flat on my stomach. This was new to me. I wasn't sure I liked this, it felt like I had much less mobility, like I was much less in control.

"And I don't want you to move, Merrin."

"I won't."

"How can I be so sure you won't?"

I felt pressure around me, physical pressure. He was straddling my hips.

"I... I promise."

He laughed. He stretched to the nightstand and I heard something getting dragged along the wood. Almost simultaneously, he lugged both my hands up in front of me, all the way to the headboard which was actually made of old timey metal posts.

"What are you doing?"

"I'm showing you who's got the power here."

Now I understood. The thing he was holding was his handcuffs!

CHAPTER 5

I was still coming to grips with what was going on when he snapped the bracelets on my wrists and around the metal bar. I was fully restrained.

"James, it's not funny!"

"It wasn't meant to be."

He touched me between the legs and the thought of closing them only occurred to me after his and fingers were worming inside my channel. By then it was too late. It felt too good to resist!

"Ooh..."

I was relishing the attention when he slipped away. This was especially disconcerting since I had my hands tied to the bed, slightly above my head. I was his prisoner, for better or for worse.

"Please, James…"

The bed shifted underneath as he moved around me. He stretched my legs apart, as far as they would go. I was more vulnerable than ever! I felt him kneel between my thighs and soon his body heat enveloped me.

"You're really looking forward to this, aren't you?"

"Yes, I need you."

He put both hands on my soft butt and kneaded the cheeks. He pinched the skin and even slapped me. It stung but I didn't do anything more than yelp. Truth was, I was enjoying this. There were tremors shooting through me.

"Aaaaahhh..."

"You like this? You like getting spanked like a dirty little whore?"

"Uh-hmmm."

His hand came faster and with more strength. He spanked me so hard that I dreaded sitting down later. But in the meantime, the stinging sensation was nothing like I'd never felt. I was getting even moister!

I don't know if the federal agent saw it but he stopped hitting me. He shuffled behind me and I felt him stretch over my body. Was he about to...? Yes, I felt the tip of his member against my mound!

"Get ready," he snarled.

I was organizing my thoughts when I felt him push into me. There was no waiting, no preparation, he rolled his hips and shoved his entire length inside of me.

"Oh!"

He didn't give me time to adjust to his considerable girth and right away he began to thrust in and out. It was all right, I was completely ready. I was slick from my arousal and entirely relaxed. It felt, so delicious! His manhood was different compared to Grayson's which was longer. Evartt had him beat in thickness and it gave me a new range of sensations to appreciate.

"You like that?" he asked.

"Yes, so much."

That was his cue for accelerating. He started to pound into me with gusto. He got his entire body into it and was basically lying on top of me. I didn't mind the pressure. If anything, it added to the experience. He reached up and caressed my stretched arms, making me aware of how helpless I was restrained like this.

"Deeper," I urged him.

He obliged, penetrating me long and deep. His stabbing couldn't quench my desire. Each plunge was akin to dipping a juicy strawberry in molten chocolate in terms of pleasure. I shivered at his touch. He was too big for my little cavity and yet I had a feeling I could have handled twice this size.

I thrashed against the headboard, pulling on my chains. He was dominating me completely and I was ashamed to enjoy it so much. He had control over me, over my body. His power was undeniable. My hunger was unquenchable.

My climax was finally at the door. The warm feeling that had been simmering in my abdomen finally exploded into sharp bolts of delight.

"Oh my God, here it comes!"

It was like I was being immersed in a lustful volcano which simultaneously dulled and heightened all my senses. I was stumbling through a dark, hazy sinkhole and my body was turning into mush. I was breathless, unprepared for the majestic orgasm even though I'd been craving it for a long time.

"Jeez," he mumbled through clenched teeth. "Get ready…"

He stiffened inside of me and I could feel my internal muscles gripping him. He pushed through and within a matter of seconds he was unleashing his boiling seed.

"Aaaahh!"

This served to rekindle my passion, stoking my fire again. I arched my back and fought against my shackles as he continued to fill me. We both became silent while we basked in our release. My curvaceous body absorbed all the pleasure he could give me.

Eventually, the tingling dwindled until it fully evaporated. The federal agent pulled out of me and stretched alongside of me. I was expecting him to leave me there or be cold to me but he quickly unlocked the handcuffs. Then, he caressed my body, from my neck to my buttocks. It was no longer sexual. It was sweet.

We remained in this position for long minutes. It might have been half an hour for all I knew. I didn't care, I was comfortable. This was a weird thing to feel. Even though Grayson had given me permission to sleep with Evartt – hell, he had encouraged me – a part of me felt as if I had betrayed him. Was it because I had enjoyed it so much? In any case, it somehow made me feel like an independent woman.

Although I desperately needed a shower, I decided to forgo it until I got home. I slid off the bed and slipped into my panties.

"So what now? You're leaving Florida?"

"Yeah, back to DC. That's how it works, you see someone for five minutes and you write a report about it for five hours."

I smiled dutifully as I picked up my dress. At least there was no awkwardness between us. This had been a passionate encounter but neither of us had any ideas about it being more than a good time. A fantastic time, I had to admit.

"Merrin, what are you doing with a guy like Grayson Holmes?"

I glanced at him but then continued slipping into my dress. "How can anyone tell why they're with the people they're with?"

"Is it the money? Are you with him because he's a billionaire, because he's powerful?"

"How dare you? I'm not that type of person, you know."

"Everybody's that type of person. You do my job long enough you realize everybody's got their price. Maybe you don't realize it but before you know it you sold out. Happens to everyone."

"Not me," I said as I pulled up the zipper while looking at myself in the mirror. "I'm with Grayson because he's nice to me, okay? Not because he buys me things or takes me places. He's nice to me and treats me well."

"He's not a good person, Merrin."

"You don't know him. All you've learned about him is from files and reports and psych profiles, right? There's no way you can know him like I do."

"But I know what he's done."

I promptly spun toward him.

"What's that supposed to mean?"

"Oh Christ," Evartt said as he sat on the edge of the bed.

He hung his head and rubbed his face as if he had already said too much.

"What? What has he done?"

"You can't tell anyone, all right? Promise me that whatever I tell you will remain between us."

"I promise," I replied without thinking. This was it, the

seduction had worked! I was finally going to learn why Homeland Security was interested in Grayson.

"Your precious boyfriend, the man who treats you so well..."

His voice trailed off and I was afraid he had changed his mind about telling me.

"Tell me, James. If this is as bad as you think it is, I need to know."

"Grayson Holmes is secretly funding terrorism."

CHAPTER 6

It was mid-morning and I'd managed to reach the Palm Beach airport just in time to see Grayson's private jet land. It helped that I hadn't been driving. No, Grayson had had his Maybach pick me up at my grandmother's place so I could meet him as he joined me in Florida.

I had called him right after I left Special Agent Evartt. However, I couldn't bring myself to share what I'd learned. Not over the phone anyway. For all I knew, I was associating with an actual terrorist. When I told him I had to have sex with the man, Grayson took it well. In fact, that's when he said he was flying down to Florida first thing in the morning.

It had been less than a week since we'd seen each other but I was taken aback by how attractive he was. How could I have forgotten so many details in so little time? He was tall and well-built – nothing like Evartt, of course. He instead had a swimmer's body which was, I had to admit, much less intimidating. He walked down from the plane and the wind caught in his sports jacket, making it billow dramatically behind him. He looked like a movie star.

"I'm so glad you came, Merrin."

Before I could answer, he reached me and took me in his arms. He crushed his mouth against mine and I was lost. Now I remembered why I had waited so restlessly next to the phone for two days. I'd missed him tremendously. I ached for him.

"Grayson, we need to talk."

"It's not all I need."

He winked at me and we didn't say anything more as the flight steward gave his luggage and briefcase to the driver who then proceeded to stow everything away in the trunk. When he couldn't wait any longer, Grayson opened the door for me and we both got in the backseat. I could never get used to this car; it was so spacious, so luxurious.

There were two leather seats in the back separated by a console which also housed a refrigerator. Once Grayson was settled in, he turned on some music, raised the electrotransparent partition screen between the driver and the rear, and pushed the button to bring out the window curtains. Within seconds, we were completely isolated from the outside world.

"I've missed you," he said.

"Me too, Grayson. I need to tell you what I learned."

"Did you enjoy using the Mata Hari approach to getting information?"

Before I could answer, I felt myself moving. It wasn't the car, I was being tilted back. Grayson was reclining my seat.

"What are you doing?"

"When I said I missed you, I meant I *missed* you. All of you."

The car started rolling and I saw through the window we were moving away from the tarmac. I glanced at the billionaire next to me and his face was becoming a mask of desire. Without ceremony, he removed his jacket.

"Did you enjoy yourself while you were being taken by a federal agent?"

"I don't wanna talk about this."

"Why? Are you ashamed?"

Truthfully, I was mad at myself for having slept with another man in the first place and having enjoyed it so much to boot. Maybe Evartt had been right when he called me a whore.

"Tell me, Merrin. Do you think I'll get mad if you admit the truth?"

"Won't you?"

"I played with myself last night as I pictured you with him."

My head snapped toward him.

"Does that shock you?" he asked.

"This is twisted."

"I love that you obeyed me, that you gave yourself to another man for me. I'm still hot for you, Merrin. Probably more than ever."

He rose from his seat and placed himself above me. He took my hand and brought it to his groin.

"Can you feel it?"

Before I could answer, he kissed me feverishly. As much as I needed time to sort out my feelings, my doubts, I was overtaken by yearning. I kissed him back with the same hunger. To be desired was a powerful aphrodisiac.

His right hand went to my chest where he proceeded to knead my heavy breasts, one after the other. The crewneck T-shirt I was wearing wasn't built for easy access but the fabric was thin enough for the warmth of his fingers to translate to my stiffening nipples.

I felt a rush of energy traveling through me, all thoughts of propriety vanishing. I stopped merely touching his crotch and began to apply pressure. He was growing in my hand, so long and hard.

"I need you," he whispered as we came up for air for an instant.

I fumbled with his belt and swiftly undid his pants. I pushed them down as well as I could from my reclining position. Then, without wasting a second, I snaked my hand through the fly of his boxers and retrieved his manhood. It was scorching at the touch!

I wanted to play with it, to do anything to please him, but he backed away a few inches. I thought he wanted to tease me but instead he reached under my loose skirt for my panties. He took hold of it and yanked back with brute force. He didn't just remove them, he ripped them off me. I was so surprised that I couldn't restrain a shriek.

He looked down at me with pure lust in his eyes. He was consumed with a fire only I could understand for I felt the same way. I wanted to kiss him again, to wrap my arms around his strong reassuring body, but there was something else on his mind.

"I'm burning for you," he said.

He grabbed my waist and pulled me down the seat a little bit. I was too big a woman to ever be comfortable having sex in the backseat of a car, even this opulent Maybach, but I was too far gone to care. I needed his touch more than I needed air right now. He lowered himself to me.

"Do it."

There was no teasing, no torturing me with what I was craving. He wiggled his shaft between my folds and rammed forward.

"Ugh!"

He filled me at once! Sheathed to the hilt, he continued playing with my breasts and he kissed me again. His sweet tongue danced with mine as he went about thrusting in and out of my tight oven.

Now that he was lower, I could finally take him in my arms. It only served to feed his passion. He slammed into me with quick strokes and I knew he wouldn't last long. Nor could I. He had awakened something within me that nothing short of an orgasm could tame.

"Yes, Grayson..."

He was controlling the speed, the depth. He was completely dominating me. I was his! He rolled his hips one more time and I felt him expand. This was it! The thought of what was going to happen triggered my release. It was like the ultimate wishful thinking.

"Oooohh!"

My climax came unexpectedly. I pulled him to me and my body was rocked by the carnal assault. My senses were aflutter, almost disconnected from reality. Right then, his stiffening reached its zenith and he flooded me.

"Aaaggh," he grunted.

He didn't stop pounding into me as we came together. The moment was beautiful, so savage and yet so intimate. I was euphoric and we each buried our faces in the other's shoulder as we rode it out. I never wanted the frenzied moment to end.

"Oh God," I whispered as time regained its properties

around us. Before he put his lips on mine I had time to mouth, "Oh Grayson…"

Even though things were over, we continued kissing for the longest time. It was tender, sweet, no longer tinted with lustful intentions. Our hunger was satisfied, for now anyway. Eventually, we pulled apart and he sat back on his seat. He didn't bother to pull up his pants and we each turned toward the other, almost as if we were in bed.

"I've missed this, Merrin. I've missed you."

I didn't answer right away. I didn't want to overextend myself because what I had to say next was vital.

"I got Special Agent Evartt to talk last night. I know why he was questioning me about you."

"Go on."

"He said… Wow, this is hard."

"It's all right, you can tell me anything."

"I'm not sure I should even be talking. I promised I wouldn't say a word to you."

"I understand, Merrin. You're in a difficult position, a position I put you in. Maybe I shouldn't have done this to you."

He reached over and caressed my hand lovingly.

"No, I'm going to tell you. I'm gonna tell you because I'm not sure I even believe what he said. It's so crazy, it can't be true. It's just…"

"What?"

"I'm afraid, Grayson. I'm afraid you could be in deep trouble."

He smiled sweetly. "Do you know how many lawyers I have on retainer? Sometimes I suspect they create trouble for me just so they can have something to do."

I smiled back but it wasn't sincere. All I could think about was how both our worlds were about to come crashing down. If I spilled the beans, things would never be the same. He patted my hand again.

"Look, I'm sorry about this. Let's pretend I didn't force you to go to bat for me. Let's pretend I didn't ask you to sleep with another man for me. Try to forget about the entire episode. I hope you'll forgive me and know that I would never do anything to hurt you, to make you feel bad."

"The guy said you're a terrorist, Grayson," I blurted out in one breath.

"What?" he exclaimed as he sat straighter.

"Special Agent Evartt said you're under investigation because he believes you're funding terrorism."

"I see."

Now it was my turn to sit up straight, putting the seat back in its original position. I looked at Grayson. He was lost in thought.

"I'm sure you can fight this, right? You can sue them for libel or slander or whatever it's called when they make false accusations."

Grayson shook his head and turned to me. "I can't do that."

"What do you mean?"

"Because these accusations are true."

*****

THE POWER BILLIONAIRE 3: SUBMISSION OF CURVES DESIRES

CHAPTER 1

A cold rain was falling on Washington DC. I had been away from the northeastern weather only a few weeks but I had already gotten used to tropical Florida. I tightened my coat and walked faster. I climbed the steps of the Georgetown brownstone and rang the bell.

"Yes?" the intercom chirped behind a veil of static.

"James, it's Merrin Rexford."

It took less than a second for the solenoid to buzz and I quickly slid inside, happy to get out of the rain. What kind of place had rain in winter anyway? If it was going to be cold, I much preferred snow.

I went up the stairs toward Special Agent Evartt's apartment. The muscular man was waiting for me with his door open. He was leaning on the door frame with his arms crossed. He was barefoot, wearing jeans and a tight, white tank top. I gulped and stopped in my tracks. He looked much better than I recalled.

Much more dangerous.

"What are you doing here?" he drawled.

"Getting out of this wet weather."

I finally got to the landing and in spite of myself I was panting. Climbing stairs was difficult for a big woman like me.

I should exercise more, I thought. Then again, exercising was difficult for a big woman like me. Damn vicious circle!

He moved aside and I went in. I was struck by how nice and clean the apartment looked. In hindsight, I shouldn't have been. I remembered his hotel room in Florida a few days ago; it had been picture-perfect with no clothes lying about. The apartment was like that, only better. There were some leather couches and armchairs making up the small living room. There were candleholders that matched antique sconces on the walls. Even the draperies harmonized the furniture.

"Let me help you with this."

Before I could answer, he was reaching in front of me from the back and unbuttoning my coat. I slid out of it and for the first time noticed the flames in the fireplace. I felt James approach behind me once again and I was afraid of doing something stupid. I escaped forward and stopped next to the crackling fire. Funny how the most intense heat was now coming from within.

"So, you traveled a thousand miles to get out of this wet weather?"

I turned to face him. He was once again leaning against a wall with his arms crossed. He reminded me of a cowboy relaxing outside of a saloon. If he'd been wearing his gun the image would've been perfect.

"I came to talk to you."

"About what?"

"You need to stop investigating Grayson. You need to tell Homeland Security to back off."

"You came here – to my home – to talk about another man? After what we did together you're asking me to look after your boyfriend?"

"You have it all wrong about him, James. He's not a terrorist. He's not funding terrorism."

He uncrossed his arms and straightened up. His jaw tightened and he was almost growling.

"Shut up about him! You can lie to yourself but you and I both know if you came here it wasn't to do him any favors.

74

You came to see me. You came to be with me."

I opened my mouth to answer but I was suddenly filled with doubt. Could this be true? Had I subconsciously volunteered to come plead Grayson's case just so I could see James again? Looking at him, my heart beat faster. He was so attractive, so feral. He was dangerous like he belonged in a Sara Fawkes novel.

"I... No, we can't be together again."

"Are you sure about that?"

Before I said anything, James was on me. His body pressed against mine, making the heat unbearable and yet making me yearn for more. His lips moved on mine and I opened my mouth to accommodate him. Our tongues danced feverishly and against my better judgment I wrapped my arms around him. I couldn't hold back, he had this power over me.

"I need you, Merrin."

His hands were all over my curvaceous body. Normally, I hated when a man let his hands roam across my plump flesh but I had no defenses against the federal agent. He took what he wanted when he wanted. And right now he obviously wanted me bad. He pinched my butt and I practically melted.

"No," I said halfheartedly. "We can't. I just came here to talk."

"There'll be plenty of time to talk after."

He kissed me again. I let my own hands wander over his well-defined chest. His muscles rippled underneath the shirt and I couldn't believe a man who looked like that could have so much desire for a woman who looked like me. It was insane, completely against the laws of nature.

For one moment I decided to accept my good fortune.

He put his hand between my legs and climbed up underneath my dress. Why had I worn this today when it was so cold? Why was I making it so easy for him?

"Oooohh..."

My misgivings vanished at once when his fingers brushed against my panties. The roughness of the lace dug between my folds at his touch. I closed my eyes and buried my face in the crook of his neck. He went on playing with me, sending bolts of pleasure through me.

"You're wet, aren't you? It's your style to gush like a whore when I'm touching you."

A few weeks ago I would have been insulted. When James spoke to me like that my brain turned to mush and it excited me. It was like he had found the secret code which unlocked my bonus features.

He was playing me with God Mode activated.

To show that I wasn't completely helpless, completely at his mercy, I dropped a hand to his crotch. I wasn't the only one who was aroused. His gigantic bulge spoke volumes and I did my very best to make it bigger, massaging it passionately.

I was losing myself to this wonderful feeling, to this depravity, when I remembered what I was doing here.

"Stop it, James. This has gone too far already."

He stopped but not like I wanted him to. He left one hand between my legs and with the other he grabbed my chin, making me look at him.

"You think so? You reckon it's gone too far?"

"Yes, there are things we need to discuss."

"You think it's gone too far like when you came to my hotel room and decided to fuck me until I spilled the beans?"

My eyes hardened. "You make it sound like I forced you. Should I remind you that you handcuffed me to the bed and spanked me?"

"Should I remind you that you enjoyed it?"

I was about to reply when he pressed his lips against mine. His tongue was halfway down my throat before I could even protest. But by then it was too late. I closed my eyes and let him have his way.

CHAPTER 2

I felt his hand move over my mound and my heart thumped faster as I expected him to give me some relief with his fingers. But no, he had something else in mind. He grabbed a handful of my underwear and tugged down violently.

"Hey!"

He pulled on my panties until they were around my knees and from there they fell around my ankles. He backed away and without warning spun me around. I had no idea what was going on and was about to speak up when he did something that gave me chills.

"What—"

He pushed me against the fireplace mantle and I had no choice but to grab it for support. At the same time, he prodded my legs apart like I was a suspect he was about to frisk.

"This is what you came here for, isn't it?" he whispered into my ear, his hot breath giving me goosebumps.

I was trapped between the brick mantle and his body which he pressed against mine. I felt his hand against my butt. He was fumbling with his belt. I knew what was coming and I should have done so much more to keep it from happening. I was weak.

I was horny.

I looked over my shoulder and saw his face twisted into a snarl. He was a man on a mission and finally I heard his pants fall to the ground. Within moments, I felt his engorged manhood quivering against my damp folds.

"You want this? You been dreaming about this?"

"Stop it, James. This has gone far enough."

"Oh yeah? I'd stop if I really believed you wanted me to

stop."

He pushed forward and the head of his thick member slipped into me. I gasped involuntarily and threw my head back.

"You still want me to stop? Just say the word."

I could practically see him smile. *Damn him for doing this to me!* It felt too good at this point to have him back away.

"Deeper," I whispered.

"What? I didn't hear you."

"Go deeper."

"You sure? A minute ago you wanted me to stop."

"Please, James. Take me!"

He licked my earlobe and rolled his hips forward. He instantly buried himself in my slick channel. I exhaled audibly as if I had just jumped into cold water on a hot summer day. He was abnormally large and he stretched me very wide. I didn't care. In fact, I loved it! It stimulated my nerve endings like nothing could.

"Like that? Is that what you want?"

"Yes! Give me more…"

He brought both hands to my chest and began to knead my hefty breasts through the fabric. His fingers dug into my soft flesh and at once I was a completely overwhelmed by his deft ministrations.

"Oh God!"

He groaned and picked up speed. He was positively ravaging me, sliding in and out and racing toward the blissful objective. Before I knew I was doing it, I leaned forward until my head rested on the mantle. This gave him a better angle for going deeper. I closed my eyes and focused on the passion that began rising in me. It started between my legs but now I could feel it everywhere.

"You want more, don't you?"

"Yes, faster…"

James propped me straight again so I was pressed against his chest. He enveloped me with his arms and pulled my stiff nipples under his fingers, through the fabric. The feeling was majestic and it took my breath away.

"I'm so close, James. So close…"

At that, he tweaked my nipples and jerked on them. It made my stomach flutter, a kind of preview of what would soon occur. All the while, he pumped faster within me, savagely showing me who was in control.

I was lost and all I could do was whimper. My eyes were tightly shut and I think my agony was turning him on. He was swelling within me as if it was possible for him to become bigger.

"Can you wait a second? Can you hold on so we can come together?"

I shook my head. What he was asking was inhuman. I was too close to voluntarily delay my climax. Only someone clinically insane would be able to do that. Could anyone resist this much pleasure?

Right then, he took my earlobe in his mouth and started sucking on the skin. How could I resist that? I was so close… so close…

"Aaaaahh!"

Suddenly, my eyes snapped open. He pulled back his tongue and bit into my ear lobe! The pain was sharp though not necessarily in a bad way. In fact, it heightened my arousal tremendously.

"That's it, right there!"

I went entirely rigid as the euphoria coursed through my body. The orgasm rocked me and I found myself humping back against James. I was vaguely aware of him hugging me more tightly and then he erupted.

"Aaaarrrggghh!" he grunted. "Take it, take it all!"

He bathed my inner walls with his frothy cream and each spurt was akin to getting stung by a needle. However, there was no pain, only extraordinary pleasure. I absorbed it silently, thrashing against the federal agent as he continued to unleash his seed.

After long minutes of this, he buried himself fully and stopped moving. His hands returned to caressing me, no longer desperate. I leaned forward again on the mantle to catch my breath and he stepped back, promptly making me feel empty, hollow. I picked up my panties and put them back in place before I made a mess and by the time I turned around James was zipping up his pants.

He looked at me and I avoided his gaze. I was actually remorseful. I had let my hormones overtake my body and now I was paying the price. I turned back toward the fire even though it was already too warm. I stared at the flames for the longest time, mad at myself and wondering how I could justify what I had done. Pleasure had a steep price.

"Here," he said. "Sorry, no pink daiquiri today."

I looked down. He was offering me a glass of whiskey. I took it and stepped away from the fireplace as I drank.

"So I guess now we can talk."

He grinned and took a sip after saying this. He sat on the wing chair, at the other end of the coffee table.

"Close the book on your investigation. Grayson isn't giving money to terrorists."

"Of course you would say that."

"He's a good man!"

"Sure, such a good man that he would send you to my hotel in Florida to seduce information out of me. He's a real stand-up guy."

"It's not like that, James."

"Merrin, please. Don't insult me."

All right, he sort of had a point. Grayson had asked me to pry the information out of the federal agent, even if I had to sleep with him. It was odd to be asked this by my boyfriend, obviously, but on the other hand I felt as if I owed him. There's a point when you feel good about doing a favor for someone and it's like you're doing yourself a favor.

"Granted, we don't have a conventional relationship, Grayson and I. But he told me the truth. I believe him."

"You know what truth is to billionaires? It's whatever they want it to be!"

"He's *pretending* to be funding terrorism. He's doing a

courtesy for the CIA, it's a sting operation. What does he get for his trouble? You on his back!"

"Of course you're gonna defend him," he said, rolling his eyes. "He's got you wrapped around his little finger like a teenage groupie tripping on Ecstasy. Open your eyes, Merrin!"

"How about you open yours?"

I slammed my glass down on the coffee table.

"Merrin..."

"You're judgmental and frankly I think you're not being impartial." It at once became clear my head. "That's it, isn't it? You're gonna pursue this because you want to take me away from Grayson. You just want a trophy!"

He stood up and pointed out the door. "Get the hell out of my house."

His eyes were smoldering with rage. I didn't waste a second grabbing my coat and leaving the apartment.

CHAPTER 3

It was still raining as I jogged down the sidewalk and crossed the street. I picked up speed as I approached the black stretch limo. Before I could get there, the rear door was opened from inside. I saw Grayson looking at me. He let go of the door and moved aside to let me in. I launched myself in, closing the door behind me.

"Are you cold?" he asked. "Do you want the heat turned on?"

"No, I'm fine."

I was more than fine. My cheeks were still burning, not only from the fire but from what James and I had done. The cold air had done nothing to cool me down. The billionaire stretched forward and knocked on the dark partition. Five seconds later, we were driving away.

"And? How did it go?"

"Not good."

"There are different degrees of not good, Merrin. How did he react when you explained to him I really wasn't funding terrorism?"

"I don't think it's too strong to say complete and utter disbelief."

"That bad, uh?"

"Yeah."

I slid on the leather and went to the minibar. My thoughts were jumbled and I needed to calm down. I desperately needed a drink. I picked the first bottle and poured myself an inch. I had drunk half of it before even knowing it was scotch.

"Hey, take it easy with that. It's all right if the ploy didn't succeed. The man is an experienced federal agent, it always was a long shot. I'm proud of you for trying."

After giving me one of his warm, comforting smiles, he came closer to me and kissed my cheek. He lingered and went down to kiss my neck when he abruptly stopped.

"Merrin? What's that sm..."

"I'd rather not talk about it, okay?"

I went back to my drink and sipped it to appear as if I was in the middle of something very important. I glanced at him and immediately noticed he was hurt. It was like I had hit him with a shovel.

"You slept with him, didn't you?"

"I said I don't want to talk about it."

"Did you do that to convince him? Did you do this for me?"

I finally turned to face him. I had never seen him like this. He seemed to have shrunk in size. The naturally tall, handsome, distinguished billionaire now looked like some insecure college freshman.

"It just happened, okay? It wasn't planned or anything. One minute I was telling him that we had to talk and the next thing I knew he was on me. For what it's worth, I told him to stop, that I didn't want to."

His head snapped up. "You told him no and he didn't listen?"

His eyes hardened and I saw his right hand ball into a fist. He was back to his dominant self and it was somewhat scary.

"It's not like that, Grayson. I didn't want to but then..."

"But then you did."

"It just happened," I repeated lamely. "I'm sorry."

He forced a smile. "You don't have to apologize. I don't own you. After what I made you to do with him in Florida, I have no business judging you."

When he had suggested I seduced James before, it had been extremely naughty. I had done so to gather information but he had admitted afterwards that it had turned him on. Lovemaking later on had been nothing short of fantastic. But tonight was of my own initiative, not his. I think that's what irked him the most. Not being in control was extremely difficult for him.

"It didn't mean anything," I said softly. "It was... It was only sexual."

"Are you sure about that, Merrin? Are you really sure about that?"

He looked at me like a high school teacher making me want to understand the error of my ways. For the first time I heard my own words. Was I really sure it had only been physical with James?

Did I have feelings for him?

* * *

The next day, my heels resounded loudly on the tiles as I struggled to keep up with Grayson's long strides. The young man leading us didn't look over his shoulder to see if we were far behind which only put additional strain on me. He looked like an intern and was probably secretly happy to have a modicum of authority for once. We turned to the right and before long the corridor veered to the left.

"Is this a maze or something?" I asked.

Grayson smiled at me. "It is, actually. They designed CIA headquarters so that the hallways are never in a straight line. It keeps the audio signals from escaping in case someone stands across the street with a microphone."

"They can do that?"

"Actually, they can't, not with this configuration. They call it The Wave."

After it seemed like we had just trekked through a national park in terms of distance, the intern led us into a conference room. Two people were already inside and they stood up. One was a balding middle-aged man in a cheap suit and the other was a woman in her late 20s. She was blonde and tall and belonged in a magazine.

"Grayson," she greeted, shaking his hand. "How are you?"

"How do you do, Rebecca? This is my friend Merrin."

"A pleasure to meet you, Merrin. I'm Rebecca Tewksbury, targeting analyst. This my superior, Robert Bozzelli."

We shook hands all around and then sat at the long table. Coffee was offered and declined and we settled into dreary chitchat. It was a windowless room so I had no choice but to focus on the two members of the Central Intelligence Agency. Bozzelli seemed bored, clearly wishing he was somewhere else, but it was the opposite for the woman.

She was all smiles and I had a sense she was flirting with Grayson. She sat several inches in retreat from the table, no doubt so the billionaire could see her flawless legs which she crossed and uncrossed every few minutes like she was auditioning for a *Basic Instinct* sequel. There was no avoiding the power of her short skirt. After five minutes I was ready to risk prison for justifiable homicide.

"Here they are," she said as the door opened.

We all stood up. The first person in was the same intern who had brought us here. Behind him was a woman in her early 50s. She was about my height and almost as plump as me. Behind her was Special Agent James Evartt. He scanned the room quickly and then kept his eyes on me. There was no hiding his surprise – his disgust? – about me being here. The intern left.

"I'm Assistant Special Agent in Charge Wiepert," the woman said before introducing James to everyone.

I dutifully shook hands with James and I had a feeling he held on a few seconds longer than customary. At the same time, his demeanor was definitely not rainbows and butterflies. He was holding me responsible for getting him dragged here.

"All right, I think we can begin," Rebecca said with a million-dollar smile.

We all sat around the table and I couldn't miss the staring contest that was going on between Grayson and James.

"As I understand it, Homeland Security has launched an investigation against Mr. Grayson Holmes. Is that correct?"

"Yes," Wiepert replied. "Special Agent Evartt is acting lead on the case."

"Right. The reason you were convened here is to ask you, in the most respectful terms, to drop this investigation."

"You know you have no authority over Homeland Security, right? You can bitch and moan and throw a hissy fit but nothing you say can legally make us stop investigating anyone."

"Did your daddy arrange this meeting?" James asked Grayson. "Must be a doozy to be the son of a U.S. Senator. He can pull all sorts of strings for you. Does Merrin know about the time you drunk drove a coed to death?"

"What?" I mumbled, turning to Grayson.

"I bet daddy came real handy that night, uh?"

"Agent Wiepert, please keep your man in line."

It was the first time Bozzelli had spoken and his voice carried authority. People subtly cleared their throats.

"The reason you're investigating Mr. Holmes is because you suspect him of funding terrorists, is that correct?"

"Yes," Wiepert answered. "We were notified of suspicious money transfers from a bank in Arizona to several offshore accounts belonging to corporations registered in Panama. We backtraced the transactions to entities belonging to Mr. Grayson Holmes."

"We're all aware of this," Rebecca said. "I have all the bank account numbers if you want to verify. We asked Mr. Holmes to route that money."

At that, James threw his head back. It was like he had just been on the receiving end of an uppercut. To be proven wrong in public was devastating to him. This is what kept me from mouthing *I told you so*.

Rebecca slid a folder across the table to the two members of a Homeland Security.

"The material before you is Eyes Only, top secret SCI level," the senior CIA man barked. "None of this leaves this room."

"Of course."

Rebecca took over. "As part of Operation Majestic Thunder, reference number 71967-AN35, we are trying to draw out insurgent elements based in Indonesia. They have links with terrorist cells in Yemen and Qatar. The mission's operational goal is to establish a fake terror network. Once it's set up, we'll have the terrorists fighting each other thinking they are actually us, the Western powers."

James and his superior followed along by looking at the paperwork in the file.

"That's..." Wiepert began, shaking her head. "That's devious."

"We're paid to be devious. Our objective is to fight a proxy war against terrorists. We'll have them doing the dirty work for us. No American lives will be lost, not anymore. We needed clean money with no ties to the U.S. government and so it was suggested by Senator Holmes, who is on the Select Committee on Intelligence, to speak with his son, a true patriot."

"If funneling $10 million can help protect my country, well, it's the least I can do."

"If you look at page 7, you'll see authorizations from DOD and the Director of Central Intelligence for these transactions."

"So we need you to drop this investigation, please," Bozzelli said. "We'll arrange it so a drug smuggler gets linked to one of the offshore accounts so you can have something to show for your time and efforts. Also, it won't appear as if you're just abandoning an ongoing investigation. Can we count on you to help us out?"

After a moment, Wiepert nodded. "Of course. Interagency cooperation is mandatory these days."

James turned to her as if he'd been stung. "But..."

"You have our *full* cooperation," she added. "From *all* our agents."

"Great!" Rebecca said, standing up to signify the meeting was over.

We all climbed to our feet and said goodbye. We filed out of the room, Grayson and I closing the ranks. I couldn't believe I had heard all that. I had been a lowly secretary for a decade and now I was hearing about secret government operations? It was surreal.

On the one hand, I was relieved that Grayson had been

telling the truth about not being really involved in terrorism. I trusted him implicitly but doubt was a dangerous thing. Now my mind was at ease. On the other hand however, this seemed dangerous. What if the terrorists learned the truth? What if they came after him?

I watched James walking ahead of us. He was clearly mad. He had been bamboozled, as Grandma Edna would say. His pride was hurt and I was afraid he would do something rash.

Right then came my worst nightmare.

CHAPTER 4

James broke free from his boss and walked back toward me. I had no choice but to stop. He looked between Grayson and me but didn't say a word yet. I knew what he wanted.

"Grayson, can you give us a minute?"

"Sure."

He glared at the federal agent for a second longer than necessary and then continued walking down the hall. He disappeared around the corner.

"What do you want, James?"

"Come stay with me, Merrin."

"Excuse me?"

"All right, so rich boy is cleaner than a new diaper after all, but I still don't trust him. He manipulates people, it's in his nature."

"And you think you telling me this will make me fall into your arms blindly?"

He surprised me by taking my hands in his and coming a little closer. It was so unexpected that I didn't back away.

"Ain't never a bad time to do a good thing. I'm hoping you can trust my word over his and see the truth, Merrin. I've... These times we spent together, it made me realize how something's missing from my life. I need someone."

"And you think that someone is me?"

"I have no doubt about this. You're smart, you're funny. You're... You're exactly my type."

"Please, I'm nobody's type."

"That's where you're wrong. You may not think much of yourself but I do. When I first saw you walking into the diner my heart nearly gave out. You're all curves and sass and right then I knew I wanted to get to know you as more than a person of interest."

"James..."

"And then you showed up at the hotel. On the one hand, I couldn't believe my luck. You were so blatantly flirting with me. It became obvious you wanted something from me. On the other hand, I didn't care, still don't. If playing along was gonna get me closer to you I was willing to do it."

"I didn't want to do it but..."

"But Holmes made you do it, I know."

"It's not like that."

"It's not? He didn't force his girlfriend to sleep with another man just so he could have a piece of information? Is that the kind of man you want to be with?"

"He didn't force me."

"Let me guess, he suggested that if you love him you'll do this for him?"

"It wasn't like that," I said instinctively despite the fact that his words rang true.

"Right, I'm sure he was much more gentlemanly about it. Tell me, did he fly into a rage when he learned you'd slept with me?"

"Of course not."

"Thank you for proving my point. He was expecting it to happen. You know why? Do you know why he wanted you to sleep with me? It wasn't so much for the information. No, he wanted to establish his dominance over you. He wanted to own you completely. Think about it, he knew that if you did that for him you'd do anything. *Anything*, Merrin! He turned you into his subservient whore."

My mouth hung open and I avoided his eyes. What if he was telling the truth? Was I being manipulated like he said? I started breathing faster and I felt my cheeks flush. And then something occurred to me. James was a cop, he was used to making accusations, used to twisting facts to get his way.

I stopped listening to his words and instead listened to what I knew. I listened to my feelings, to my heart. While James had the gist of the situation in a very clinical way, he didn't know about the nuances. He didn't know about the context or the people involved.

He didn't know about *me*.

I yanked my hands out of his and looked at him again. "You think you have it all figured out, don't you?"

"It's a pretty easy situation to figure out, Merrin."

"No, it's not. You may think you know about what we did, about our relationship, but you're missing the most important piece of the puzzle."

"Which is?"

"Feelings, kindness, history."

"Okay, fine. You have a point." He came close again and dropped his voice. "This doesn't change the fact that I know about *my* feelings. I can't stop thinking about you. I want to be with you."

"James…"

"Don't cut me off, I know you have feelings for me, too. Maybe I can't convince you to hate the other guy but maybe I can convince you to love me. The things we did together, ain't just anybody gonna put up with it like you did. We're… We're compatible, Merrin. You can't deny this."

He had a point. When he took me I felt like a different woman. I melted under his touch. He was so dominant, so dangerous, it never failed to inflame me. There was some of this with Grayson but with James it was much more… raw. Compatibility sure wasn't a problem between us.

"I want you to think about this," he continued. "Search your feelings, you know I'm right. We go together like Cupid and arrows."

Before I could react, he leaned down toward me. I was afraid he would crush his lips against mine and that would make me lose it completely. But instead, he brought his lips to my ear.

"I don't think I can live without you, gorgeous."

He kissed me on the cheek, gave me one last look, and walked away. I remained there motionless, merely staring at the floor. Why did life have to be so difficult?

"Are you all right?"

I glanced up and found Grayson walking back toward me. There was worry in his eyes.

"Yes, I'm fine."

It was a big fat lie and I prayed he wouldn't notice that my eyes were watering.

"You know, they say the way the corridors are set up it makes it harder to eavesdrop. I think they have to reevaluate. I heard a good chunk of your conversation with Special Agent Evartt."

"All of it?"

He nodded. "What mattered anyway. Did you take his words seriously?"

"He was pretty sincere."

"And what do you think about all this?"

"What am I supposed to think, Grayson? A man just basically threw himself at my feet. That's not something that happens to a girl like me, like ever."

"I see."

"What?" I asked at his enigmatic comment.

"You didn't turn him away outright. That's... telling."

"What do you mean?"

"I mean the federal agent clearly has stated his case. I won't say anything against that. I just hope that my sincerity isn't something you can dismiss readily."

That's when I remembered something that had been said during the meeting.

"Grayson, what did he mean when he talked about you being involved with a dead coed?"

He looked away and sighed. He took a step back and I followed him. Before long, we were walking toward the exit.

"That was a long time ago."

"Tell me anyhow."

"It was my sophomore year at Harvard and we were coming back from a party. There were five of us and we were all drunk out of our skulls. I was in the back, in and out of consciousness. Eventually I woke up in the hospital and I learned that we'd been in an accident. My roommate's girlfriend had died. It wasn't my car, I wasn't driving. Evartt just wanted to rattle your cage."

"It worked."

"Not too much, I hope. I'm sure you know the future would be a lot brighter with me."

"We're talking about the future now?"

"Of course. Merrin, I love you."

I stopped in my tracks and he didn't have a choice but to do the same thing. I glared at him in a way I never thought I would.

"How can you say such a thing?"

"It's the truth, I can't deny my feelings."

A part of me was ecstatic. Rich, handsome, powerful, and in love with me? Anyone would have killed to be in my position. I thought back of my first real boyfriend in high school and how I'd stayed up at nights praying that he would say he loved me. Ultimately, he'd dumped me before I could hear these words.

However, something else was nagging at me.

"Great timing, Grayson."

"What do you mean? I don't understand."

"Are you springing this on me because you want to upstage James?"

He snorted. "That's ridiculous."

"Is it? It's so convenient. You declare your love five minutes after James says he wants me to be with him?"

"It's a coincidence, don't read any more into it than that."

"I think I should. I think you have an ulterior motive. It's as if you're saying this just because you want to win. You're so used to getting your way that you won't let me entertain being with someone else."

"Are you?"

"Am I what?"

"Are you entertaining being with him? Seriously?"

"To tell you the truth, I am now."

He tried to put his hand on my shoulder but I shook it off. I turned around and walked around quickly.

CHAPTER 5

I barely said two words to Grayson as we drove back into the city and to the hotel. I knew he was staring at me, hoping I would allow our conversation to resume but I looked out the window and did my best to gather my thoughts. More precisely, I did my best to blank out my mind.

Epic failure.

Once in the hotel suite, I gathered my things and threw them in my overnight bag. Perhaps I was being a tad dramatic but I desperately needed to be alone. I desperately needed to think.

"I'll make my own way down to Florida," I said as I headed for the door.

"Merrin—"

I didn't hear the rest over the sound of the door slamming behind me. What had I just done? Had I just turned my back on the one man who had ever made me feel special? No, he was the second man.

Geez, I don't know anymore…

I went down and caught a taxi. When the driver asked me where I was going I was completely at a loss. I was such a great planner! Not knowing where I was going exactly, I told him to bring me to the airport.

"Reagan or Dulles?"

"The one that flies to Florida."

"Reagan then."

This was a brash decision. I didn't know if there were flights available or if I even had enough money to buy a ticket. I pulled out my phone, remembering that this wasn't 1950 and I could book a flight with a couple of keystrokes.

And then I had a better idea.

I dialed a number, for once not caring about long-distance fees.

"Hello? Is this the go-go stripper calling?"

"No, it's me, Grandma."

"Merrin?" she asked as if she had more than one granddaughter.

"What was that about strippers?"

"Today is the birthday of Glenda Mickunas, up on the seventh floor? She's turning 87, good complexion for her age. She's lucky she's a redhead, you can't tell the liver spots from her freckles. The girls of the Senior Center are chipping in to get one of them go-go strippers. I thought it was him calling to get directions. I need to talk to him before the show, we wanna ask him if he's comfortable doing things with pudding pops."

I closed my eyes and shook my head, picturing my 79-year-old grandmother waving a dollar bill around. I sincerely hoped she wasn't thinking about licking pudding off anybody.

"That's great, Grandma. I'm sure you'll have an excellent time."

"Do you..." she began, dropping her voice. "Do you know if you can catch one of them venereal diseases by stuffing money down a G-string?"

"No, I think you're safe."

"Good, good. The girls were wondering about that. I'll need to stop at the cash machine before the party then."

"Hmm, have fun," I said weakly.

"Merrin, you all right?"

"Not really, to be honest."

"What's wrong? You're not in the family way, are you?"

"No! It's nothing like that. It's just... It's..."

"Boy trouble, uh?"

I glanced at the cab driver to make sure he wasn't eavesdropping and discovered he had ear buds firmly inserted.

"Got any advice?"

"Depends what the problem is. Is it that you're not getting satisfied? I hear that happens, you know. Them young rich

96

guys look really virile but couldn't drill a hole in a watermelon if their lives depended on it. Saw that on *Donahue* back in the 80s. Very risqué material back then."

"That's not the problem, believe me. There are two men now. They're sort of competing for me."

"And that's a problem?"

"I know, right? But I'm not living it a commune. I have to pick one. Or neither. It's… complicated, Grandma."

"Who says you have to pick? You like them both? Try them on!"

"I have," I answered sheepishly.

"Oh. Together, at the same time? Had a friend back in the Korean War, Annette Rostkowski, she found herself being courted by two beaus. She liked them both equally. One night she had too much sherry to drink and had both men joined her in her rooming house. Long story short, things got hot and heavy and she found out suitor number one was actually interested in suitor number two. My point is, if she hadn't brought them to her room together she never would've found out he was a swish!"

"We say gay now, Grandma."

"Fine, he was a gay. All I'm saying is maybe you have to test them out thoroughly to find out which one you wanna be with."

Although I wasn't about to admit it to her, I had tested Grayson and James pretty thoroughly already. Neither was gay so that point was moot.

"I can't pick and it's driving me insane. I like them both, for different reasons, but I still feel I owe it to them to pick one."

"Merrin, I only see one solution to your problem."

"What?" I asked, fully expecting another nonsensical anecdote.

"Close your eyes and pretend you can't see either of them ever again. Think about which one you would miss the most."

That strangely made a lot of sense. For her wackiness, my grandmother could be very deep sometimes.

"Thank you, Grandma."

"That's what I'm here for. Now, what flavor do you think the go-go stripper would prefer to lick off Glenda Mickunas's droopy boobs? Chocolate or butterscotch?"

I laughed and a minute later I was hanging up. If anything, I could always count on Grandma Edna to cheer me up.

I returned to staring out the window. I saw parents walking around with their giggling children. I saw teenage couples holding hands, visibly wondering if it was too soon for that first kiss. I saw toddlers running after puppy dogs and then beating retreat when the pet decided to give chase.

What all of these had in common was the absence of loneliness. This was a feeling with which I was well acquainted. I'd been on my own more often than not throughout my life. Women of my size hadn't been popular in over a century and this solitude had been especially difficult during my teenage years.

Did I really want to be alone again?

I closed my eyes and devoted serious brainpower to what my grandmother had told me. Which one would I miss the most if I could ever see them again? They were both handsome, though in different ways. They were both fantastic lovers, so raw and powerful. So dominating.

Who couldn't I live without?

My eyes flew open. The choice was clear.

"Change of plans," I told the driver. "We're going to Georgetown."

I was going to see James.

CHAPTER 6

After the taxi dropped me off I buzzed James's apartment but of course he was still at work. I waited over half an hour by the door and when an elderly lady slipped out to walk her poodle I let myself in. I climbed to his floor and sat on the ground. I waited. A few people glanced at me in a funny way as they walked by but I was mostly left alone.

It took over two hours before James appeared. He spotted me from the bottom of the steps and stopped. I stood up and he hurried up to join me.

"Merrin!"

"Hey, James. I came here to talk to you."

"You been waiting long?"

"Doesn't matter."

Although he was doing his best to conceal it, he was starting to smile. He looked so handsome, so endearing. He went next to me and unlocked his door.

"Come inside, I'll mix some drinks. Bought everything required to make pink daiquiris this morning."

"If it's all right, I'd rather do this here."

"Do what?"

"James, I came to tell you that we can't see each other anymore."

"Did he put you up to this?"

"Nobody put me up to anything. I like you, okay? I like you a lot."

He gently touched my arm. "Be honest. We're way past the like phase."

"James…"

"We're compatible, you and me. I know how I make you

feel when we're together. You can't deny that."

"Physically, yes. The way… the way you touch me… it's quite something. But I finally realized that I don't *love* you. As much as I'd want to, I could never love you. I'm sorry it has to be this way."

"I don't believe you. He has you under some sort of spell or something."

"Maybe you're right, James. In any case, it's a spell I want to be under. I choose… I choose him."

I put my hand on his shoulder and debated giving him a kiss on the cheek. In the end, I decided it would send him the wrong signal.

"Goodbye," I said before turning around and leaving.

* * *

I was told at the hotel that Grayson had already checked out. My heart nearly gave out. How could I have been so stupid? Why couldn't I see how clear things had been before? The man at the reception desk told me the limo had taken him to the airport.

I rushed out and took a taxi. I promised all the money I had on me if the driver could take me to Reagan National in record time. The young man took that as a challenge and the tires screeched at every corner as we made our way to Arlington, Virginia for the second time today. Once I got there, I had to go through TSA checkpoints and they kept looking at me suspiciously. Apparently, nervous people in airports make them nervous in return. Go figure.

All the same, I was finally released. I rushed out on the tarmac where a jet with the Holmes family crest was painted on the tail. TSA had to announce me so Grayson was standing halfway down the stairs. The look on his face was unreadable.

"Hi, Grayson."

"Come inside, it's freezing out here."

I followed him up the stairs and into the plane. I dropped my overnight bag on the closest seat and noticed he was waiting for me next to the plush leather couch. He politely motioned for me to sit. After I complied, he sat at the other end of the sofa.

"I'm really glad to see you, Merrin. It's hard for me to accept people not doing what I want them to do. I'm working on that."

"I know."

That made him grin.

"I just came back from James's apartment," I continued.

His jaw tightened and he was basically bristling. "I see."

"I told him I couldn't see him anymore. I told him he isn't the man for me."

"And is there? A man for you, I mean."

"Yes. Grayson, I did a lot of thinking. My body has made a lot of decisions lately but today it was time for my brain to sort things out. It was time for my heart to speak."

"And?"

"Turns out it's a no-brainer. The only person I want to be with is you."

His lips parted in anticipation and he slid closer to me. "Merrin…"

"My grandmother – I called her earlier – she made me realize that I don't know what I'd do without you. I close my eyes and I imagine a life without you in it, and all I can see is misery. I would miss your kindness and your take-charge attitude. I would miss the way you look at me and make me push my boundaries. When I'm with you I feel like the best woman and I can ever be. Grayson, I love you."

He looked at me with wide eyes and I could practically see his heart swell. He was stunned and completely happy. I knew how he felt because I was undergoing the same emotions. We wrapped our arms around each other simultaneously and our lips hurriedly met.

We kissed long and hard. I was hungry for him and by his vigor it was obvious he felt the same way. I couldn't believe how I could have doubted my feelings for him. I knew now that he was right for me, we were a perfect fit.

"Are you ready to go? Do you need to get something back at the hotel?"

I shook my head. "I have everything I need right here."

"So do I."

He turned toward the galley and cockpit. "We're ready for takeoff, guys!"

He stood up and took my hand. I climbed to my feet and let him lead me to the back where the master suite was laid out. We went in and he closed the door behind us. The place wasn't even as large as a cheap motel room but it was perfect for what I had in mind.

"Come here," I whispered.

I took him in my arms again and we made out fiercely. I let my hands roam up and down his chest and on the upswing I took hold of his jacket which I then proceeded to slide down his shoulders. Not only didn't he stop me but he did the same with my coat.

Once it hit the floor, he started working on the front buttons of my dress. I closed my eyes and let him do it. There was urgency in his fingers. My heart was beating faster as I thought about what would happen soon. To keep myself from going insane, I started working on unbuttoning his shirt.

We disrobed each other silently, peppering our movements with soft kisses. He was the first to remove his shirt and I responded by taking off my shoes. He let his pants fall to the ground and I removed my dress. I was wearing a slip to hide my midsection. He knew I wouldn't go any further so he removed his shoes and pushed down his underwear.

"Oh wow..."

He was already erect and it made me lick my lips absentmindedly. His manhood was long and proportionally wide. It brought back so many great memories. There was a glint in his eye as he saw me observing him. He winked and then turned down the covers of the bed.

"Wait."

"What is it?"

"I want... I want to show you everything."

Taking a deep breath to make sure I would go through with this, I grabbed the hem of the slip and yanked it off my head. It was the first time I was truly revealing my plump body to him in daylight. A part of me wanted to run away screaming but the way he was watching me told me he was in heaven. There was no judgment, no repulsion.

"Thank you for this, Merrin."

He took me in his arms and kissed me deeply. I felt his shaft digging into my tummy and I promptly found myself starved for it. After a minute, we moved together toward the bed and laid down on it.

There was a soft knock at the door. "Mr. Holmes? Please strap yourselves in, we're about to take off."

There were a couple of captain's chairs with the necessary seatbelts. I was about to get out of bed when Grayson held me back.

"Let's hold onto each other instead."

He held me by the waist and had the other arm behind my shoulders. I reciprocated and the serenity in his eyes translated to me. I barely felt the plane taxi down the runway. He kissed me, full of love and tenderness. He tasted so good, so manly, that all my apprehensions vanished.

All of a sudden, the jet rose and we were tilted back. There was pressure but we couldn't slide further than the headboard. We were pushed into the mattress as we got off the ground and passed the time by making out. Before long, we were leveling off.

"Now we can begin having some real fun," he said.

"Too bad for you, I've been having fun since I climbed aboard."

He actually raised an eyebrow at that. I was much more assertive than usual and I wasn't even ashamed. I kissed him quickly, hot and wet, and disengaged myself from him. I pushed on his shoulders so he would recline and then I moved back on all fours.

"What are you doing?"

For sole answer I winked.

CHAPTER 7

I was now between his legs and his member was conspicuously in front of me. It was throbbing lightly and I blew on it in passing. I circled it with a finger, touching it in feather-like fashion. I heard his voice catch in his throat. It made me smile.

I cast my eyes down and focused on his long erection. I held it in my hand and tightened my grip. Little by little, I brought my head down.

"Merrin, you don't... You don't have to do this."

"I know."

This was probably why I wanted to go through with it. He wasn't forcing me into doing anything. It was evident that for once there was no mind games, no control issues. He wanted me to be happy no matter what.

I closed the distance and took him in my mouth. There was no frenzied passion like that last time James had forced me to suck him off. I was approaching this as making love. My tongue glided along his length and I tasted him down there for the first time. It was divine! I should have done that a long time ago.

"Oh God..."

I looked up and found Grayson with his head digging into the headboard, his eyes closed and his hands balled into fists. I was obviously doing something right. I closed my own eyes and gave myself to the experience. I inhaled him deeply and let my head move up and down while my hands caressed his strong thighs and washboard abs.

"Hhmmm, Merrin..."

I laved him hungrily and didn't even flinch when he started

leaking over my tongue. I swallowed and continued, going faster over his magnificent rod. All of a sudden, I felt pressure on my head. I had flashbacks of James shoving my head down on him and panicked for a second.

Grayson was brushing my hair away, no doubt so he could watch what I was doing to him. He kept his hand close but mostly it was cradling my neck, quietly stroking me. My tension vanished and I went back to discovering how fellatio could be extremely sensual in the right circumstances.

"Feels so good."

Indeed, I thought. I could see myself doing more of this in the near future. I squeezed him in my hand and lazily pumped him to match the rhythm of my mouth.

"Merrin, stop. Stop!"

I quickly let go and looked up at him. "Is everything okay?"

"It's more than okay. That's the problem. I don't want to race to the finish line. Come here."

He took my upper arms and pulled me to him. In spite of my weight, he swiftly brought me to him and I literally crashed onto his chest. He lifted my chin, gazed lovingly into my eyes, and kissed me. It was sweet and soft and what convinced me the most of his genuine affection was that he didn't think twice about where my mouth had just been.

I practically dissolved against him as we continued kissing. I was prepared to spend the entire flight doing only that when the plane hit a pocket of turbulence. It wasn't strong and it didn't last long but it was like being in a washing machine.

"Good thing you didn't have me in your mouth just then," he said with a smile.

I blanched as I realized what could have happened and that made Grayson laugh heartily.

"Relax, this high-wire stuff only makes it better."

He gave me a quick smooch before sliding out from under me. In the process, he made me lie on my back. He kissed my neck, my shoulder, and went down to my breasts. He took them into his hands and massaged them sensually, letting his thumbs circle the pink areolas. This was unnecessary since my nipples were already stiff with desire.

He took them into his scorching mouth as he journeyed further down. His tongue offered languorous strokes before he sucked them proper. I felt tingles zipping down to my belly! While still in this position, he ran his fingers along my folds, enjoying the smooth, warm dampness which I couldn't conceal from him.

"Oooohh…"

My desire swelled and I involuntarily raised my hips a little, encouraging him to explore me further. He kissed his way down and at the same time his fingers slipped inside. They plunged deep, making me inhale sharply. He used his other hand – the palm, to be precise – to rub the length of my slit. I had to suppress a moan, unwilling to show him how much I was at his mercy.

He teased my love button out of hiding and then blew cold air on it, making me shiver in arousal. I looked down at him and he was staring right back, seemingly asking permission to go on or, more likely, wanting me to agonize.

"Do it," I urged.

With a grin, he dipped his head and put his mouth on me. He licked in broad strokes, carefully lapping up my juices while he did corkscrew motions with his fingers. I closed my eyes and basked in the mind-blowing sensation. I absentmindedly brought a hand to my chest in order to knead my heavy breasts and the other hand went down to Grayson's head. I ran my fingers through his hair and pushed down, willing him to go faster, to send me over the edge.

He lavished attention on every square inch of my womanhood. He kissed and sucked and licked, simultaneously using his hands to work up my erect nub. My body reacted by writhing against the mattress and there was no stifling my whimpers.

His agile tongue darted in and out of me for long, unmerciful minutes. A part of me didn't think I could take any more of it but at the same time I wanted this to last forever. While he continued to fondle me, he crept farther up and locked his lips around my clit, making his tongue swirl around it.

"Oh God!"

His resolve was barbarous! I couldn't think, I couldn't breathe, I could barely remain conscious as his fingers worked in tandem with his tongue. I brought a hand to my mouth and bit on my knuckles hoping that the pain would bring me back to my senses. It didn't. It couldn't!

I was on the threshold of a fierce and jubilant trip to cloud nine. *Yes… Just a little more…*

And then Grayson stopped.

"No!" I complained. "Go back, please!"

He smirked at my panicked disposition and crawled up my body. All my disappointments vanished when he mashed his mouth against mine. I tasted myself on his lips but didn't give it a second thought. If anything, it made the heat blaze between my legs even more. It was so naughty, so deliciously lewd.

"I want you, Merrin."

"Yes…"

"Do you want me too?"

"Oh God, take me! I can't wait, Grayson. Take me now!"

He shifted to get into a proper angle and I took the opportunity to spread my legs. I even lifted them to the point where I looked like a baby going through a diaper change. This was another act of raunchiness and it wasn't lost on him. Before long, I felt his tumescent shaft sliding up and down my wet mound.

His hardness was enjoyable as it rubbed along the moist folds. Yet, I wanted more. I wanted to experience the whole package, for the two of us to become whole. I touched his face, tracing the contours of his cheekbones and strong jaw.

"I want you in me."

Without a word, he rolled his hips, thrusting into me. I gasped and threw my head back! He filled me so exquisitely, spreading me wide open. He continued on, sinking all the way in, and I wanted him to push on forever. Being completely stuffed wasn't enough.

I let out a deep groan while bracing myself for his movements within me. He was obviously taking his time to optimize my experience but I had other ideas. I was greedy for his body, I longed to be ravished and tormented.

"You're so wet, Merrin."

I took that as a compliment and smiled. *Oh yes*, I was excited!

"You make me that way."

He kissed me and at once pulled out before propelling himself into me again. I moaned in surprise as he bottomed out. My hands glided down his body to his perfect butt and with carefully timed squeezes I urged him to drill me faster, harder.

"Hhmmm…"

My gesture was working. I felt his erection quivering inside of me, hitting the velvety surface of my channel to the point where I positively wanted to scream. He bore into me with purpose, no longer merely focusing on my pleasure but working on his and well. I didn't mind, I was right up there with him.

"Oh, Merrin! Oh, won't be long…"

His words were music to my ears. I was on the brink myself. The attention he bestowed on me was bearing fruit. My skin was beginning to prickle, the heat was spreading way past the borders of my apex.

"Yes, more!"

He gave me a faint smile and then crushed his lips against mine. He sucked on my tongue, it was so intimate and tender. His kiss was threatening to send me over the edge the most. His manhood pistoning within me, his broad chest sweeping along my hard nipples, they were all great but it was his lips that made my heart light.

He went faster and a less lubricated person would have been in danger of catching fire. The trembling of the airplane made his member touch me in places he never otherwise could have reached. I hugged him tightly to me and the waves of pleasure started to focus to a sharp point.

"Grayson…" I whispered as I broke the kiss. "Oh Grayson…"

I buried my face in his neck and that's when the ferocious avalanche charged upon me. I was positively delirious as my body became overloaded with sensory stimuli. It was like I was floating while under the influence of a very powerful narcotic.

"Here it is," he grunted.

I barely heard him speak but there was no escaping what he was doing to me. He swelled within my channel and almost instantly he was erupting. He sprayed torrentially against my inner walls and it only served to heighten my blissful rapture. Now it was his turn to hide his face in my neck even though the angle was more difficult for him. I felt his warm breath in my ear.

We came and came again, together as one. I dug my nails into his back without realizing it. He didn't budge, completely lost in the tempestuous euphoria that overwhelmed us both. I continued thrashing against him and he held on to me firmly, unwilling to let me go.

After what seemed like forever, we stopped moving. He remained inside of me; I would have been disappointed otherwise. We were out of breath but in no way indisposed. He kissed my cheek and trailed his way to my mouth. I parted my lips and welcomed him eagerly.

"I don't ever want to lose you, Merrin."

"Me neither."

"I could lose all my money, all my belongings, all my influence, all my power and it wouldn't matter at all if you were still by my side. The one thing I know for certain is that you are the love of my life."

I was mad at myself because my eyes were getting watery. No one had ever said something as sweet to me before.

"Grayson, how can you say such a thing? How can you love someone like me?"

"How can I not? You're perfect for me. Are you crying?" He wiped a tear away with his thumb. "Why are you crying?"

"Because I've never been so happy, Grayson. I love you so much."

His worried face switched to a smile and he kissed me again. We were locked by our lips.

We were locked by our hearts.

THE END

If you enjoyed it, don't be afraid to leave reviews and share on Twitter!

ABOUT THE AUTHOR

Angelina Spears thrives on crafting stories that will take readers on a wild ride, emotional and physical. Having discovered her love of writing at a young age, she is never as happy as when she makes characters fall into imminent danger while dealing with romantic turmoils.

There are days when her writing is fast and hard against the washing machine but mostly she prefers candlelight and soft music by the fireplace. Champagne and strawberries, anyone? She divides her time between the cold north and sunny southern shores.

You can visit her at AngelinaSpears.com

Subscribe to Angelina's newsletter today!

CHECK OUT MORE STORIES FROM
ANGELINA!

DON'T MISS SMUGGLER!

AngelinaSpears.com

The best of romance!

CPSIA information can be obtained
at www.ICGtesting.com
Printed in the USA
BVHW031728170219
540474BV00001B/76/P

9 781480 211476